ORCA BOOK PUBLISHERS

National Library of Canada Cataloguing in Publication Data

Bennett, Holly, 1957-
The bonemender / Holly Bennett.

ISBN 1-55143-336-2

I. Title.

PS8603.E62B65 2005   jC813'.6   C2005-903300-2

Summary: In this fantasy, Gabrielle is a bonemender, a healer, who falls
in love with a man whom fate seems to have forbidden her, but they
must both think about war before they can think about love.

First published in the United States 2005
Library of Congress Control Number: 2005927810

Orca Book Publishers gratefully acknowledges the support for its publishing programs
provided by the following agencies: the Government of Canada through the Book
Publishing Industry Development Program (BPIDP), the Canada Council for the Arts,
and the British Columbia Arts Council.

Cover artwork, cover design, interior map: Cathy Maclean
Typesetting: Lynn O'Rourke

In Canada:	**In the United States:**
PO Box 5626, Stn. B	PO Box 468
Victoria, BC Canada	Custer, WA USA
V8R 6S4	98240-0468
www.orcabook.com	*www.orcabook.com*

09 08 07 06 05 • 5 4 3 2 1
Printed and bound in Canada
Printed on 100% post-consumer recycled paper,
100% old growth forest free, processed chlorine free using vegetable, low VOC inks.

To my three sons, Riley, Jesse and Aaron,
who turned me into a fantasy nerd.

ACKNOWLEDGEMENTS:

The song Gabrielle sings is inspired by "The Bergen," by the fine British singer/songwriter Jez Lowe. Thanks for his kind permission to excerpt a snippet of the lyrics.

Special thanks are due to my son, Aaron, who patiently listened to this story as it was written and thus became my first-round editor, and to my niece, Keegan—Gabrielle's biggest fan—who has read *The Bonemender* draft more often than I have. Thanks also to my agent, Lynn Bennett, and to my editor, Maggie deVries at Orca Book Publishers, for being tough on sloppy writing in the kindest possible way and for the wonderful enthusiasm she brought to our work together.

CHAPTER 1

"**B**ONEMENDER'S here, son."

The boy's face was pinched with pain, pallid under his shock of black hair. He glared at Gabrielle and hunched over his left arm, which he cradled in his other hand. He was frightened of her, of what was to come.

Gabrielle knelt beside the boy. She smiled at him. "Hello, Philippe. That must hurt like fury." He bit his lip, nodded. The blue eyes were trying to fill with tears, but he blinked them away. "Can I look?" asked Gabrielle. "I promise not to touch it."

Philippe glanced at his mother—who nodded firmly—hesitated, then stared at Gabrielle with a look of cool appraisal that was unnerving in one so young. She returned his gaze, allowing him to take her measure. With a tiny nod, he revealed his injury.

It looked awful. An angry lump jutted forward from the boy's chest, the arm hanging, useless. Poor Margot must have been frightened to death at the sight, thought Gabrielle. She sat back on her heels.

"Listen, Philippe. This is not as bad as it looks," she said. "You've dislocated your shoulder joint, but if the bone is not broken it can be easily fixed. You will mend as well as ever." The boy's eyes searched her face. "I need to check if there is anything else wrong. I'm going to just run my hand lightly along your arm, all right? I'll do my very best not to hurt you." Another nod, this one less reluctant.

Gabrielle laid her hand lightly on Philippe's skinny arm just below the swollen shoulder joint. She worked her way down the bones, feeling for bumps, swelling, odd angles. Besides the nasty scrapes, there was nothing obvious. She asked Philippe to move his fingers, then his wrist. He could move the elbow joint up and down. He wouldn't try it sideways, but that was because of the pain it caused in his shoulder.

"You were lucky, my boy. Falling from a roof like that, you could have broken bones all over the place. You must be like a cat, to land so well." Gabrielle grinned, further disarming her patient. It was not only kindness that prompted her; the treatment would be easier if Philippe was relaxed enough to cooperate. Despite himself, Philippe smiled. He was proud of his little escapade, though he would undoubtedly be punished for it once he recovered.

"Philippe," said Gabrielle, serious now. She looked him right in the eye. "I have to move your arm back into the place in your shoulder where it fits." She showed him on her own shoulder how it would be done. "I won't lie to you—it's going to hurt. But it won't take long, and when I'm done, your arm will feel a whole lot better. If I don't do it, it will never heal on its own."

Philippe's eyes teared up again, but he didn't hesitate. "Okay. You c'n do it."

Gabrielle first gave him a tea of comfrey, willow bark and hawkweed, sweetened with honey. "This will help you heal faster. It will help you sleep too, and that's the best thing you could do this afternoon." Drinking the tea also gave the boy a little reprieve, a chance to relax and prepare himself. When he was done, Gabrielle had him lie on his pallet. Holding the arm above the elbow steady with one hand, she raised his hand to point at the ceiling. Then she brought his wrist, slowly and smoothly, in an arc away from his body and down to the floor. Philippe cried out, the tears unchecked now. Then, with a clunk, the bone slid back into place. Philippe stopped crying and stared at Gabrielle, astonished.

"Is it done?" It was Margot, his mother, as incredulous as her son.

"Yes," Gabrielle replied with a smile. "I'll stay for a while, if I may, and help the torn tissues mend. It will speed his recovery. But I expect your main trouble now will be keeping him quiet for the next few days. He'll need to keep that arm in a sling, and avoid jostling it, until it's well set." Margot turned her back and busied herself with a kettle, hiding her tears of relief. She too had feared for her son.

Gabrielle tied up the sling and accepted a cup of tea from Margot. The two women chatted quietly until Philippe, exhausted, fell asleep. Then Gabrielle got back to work. She knelt by the boy once more, cupped her hand over his injured shoulder. She let her eyes close, her breathing deepen and slow. With her mind still and focused, Gabrielle sent her awareness flowing down to the swollen, torn tissues. Her hand tingled as the warm light flowed through her. The world around dimmed, until there was nothing but the small body under her hand, the light and the healing. She "saw" the muscles knit themselves, firming around the joint. The angry swelling melted away as the light infused the boy's shoulder.

She sat thus for half an hour, until she was sure the injury would heal fast and trouble-free. Then she sighed, straightened and slowly brought herself back.

"Keep him quiet for as long as you can, Margot, and give him that tea twice a day for three or four days. You can wash the scrapes with it too," she said. "He's going to be fine."

"Bless you, Lady Gabrielle."

THE NOONDAY SUN pierced through the woodland, creating dramatic shafts of green light in the shady stillness and dappling the backs of the two travelers. Their horses walked at ease, cropping now and then at a tuft of grass but needing no urging from the riders to keep moving along the trail. Indeed, they appeared to need no direction at all—the riders used neither saddle nor rein to guide their steeds. The woods were lazy at this time of day, with few birdcalls or other sounds save the clopping of the horses' hooves and the occasional murmur of the companions' voices.

One rider, golden-haired, shaded his eyes and pointed left of the trail.

"Féolan, there's a glint of water there. Maybe a stream?"

The horses stopped, and the riders sat silent, listening. The chatter of water flowing over rocks was unmistakable. Danaïs grinned modestly.

"You saw it first, Danaïs, and I owe you a dinner tonight if we're lucky enough to find an inn," Féolan said. "Let's fill up our skins, and see if our little stream lends itself to a wash and a rest."

The two men dismounted and untied the water skins draped over the horses' backs. Féolan spoke briefly in his horse's ear, and they headed into the woods, horses following.

The stream proved brisk and clear, though too overgrown on its banks to provide the hoped-for bask in the sun. They filled the skins, stripped off their boots and cooled their feet in the water. The horses waded in gratefully and drank. But there was little reason to linger. "Might as well push on," said Danaïs, brushing twigs and pine needles off his feet. "The sooner we leave, the sooner we reach the next town. I intend to have a heroic appetite by nightfall." He started making his way back, whistling merrily. He could literally whistle the birds out of the trees and often did so for his young daughter's amusement.

Féolan took a last drink, splashed his face with water and secured the skins on the horses' backs. As he turned to follow Danaïs, he saw, rather than heard, the underbrush rustling with the flight of some great creature and shouted out a warning even as he knocked an arrow to his bow and began tracking its path. Danaïs, quick though he was, barely had time to turn his head. A cry of dismay burst from Féolan's throat as the boar shot from the thicket and charged at his friend. The bow sang, but in vain. No arrow on earth could stop three hundred pounds of hurtling boar. Groaning, he watched the enraged beast crash against Danaïs, lunging viciously with its tusks.

GABRIELLE HUMMED TO herself as she ambled up the dusty road back to the castle. She loved her work, but less so when it required hurting patients. She was glad Philippe had been so easily mended. She nodded to Yves, the gatekeeper, as she ducked through the arched entrance.

"G'day, Lady Gabrielle. That Delacroix boy going to be all right, is he?"

"Yes, Yves. Just a dislocation, luckily. It looked worse than it was." Crusty old Yves had kept the gate for as long as Gabrielle could remember and seemed to know the news almost before it happened. How he had learned about Philippe's accident was anyone's guess.

"That lad's a spunky one. I'll wager you'll be tendin' him again afore he's grown."

Gabrielle laughed. "You may be right. Only eight years old, on the roof!" She started across the courtyard and was nearly at the castle doors when a clatter of hooves and a startled cry from the gatehouse made her turn around.

A man—no, two men on a single horse were cantering up to the gatehouse, a second horse trailing after. One of them shouted as he approached.

"Please help me! My friend's been hurt; he's bleeding badly. Please, is there someone who can help?"

Gabrielle saw then that the forward man was slumped against the other, his leggings black and dripping with blood. She was back at the gatehouse and clipping out orders before the bemused Yves had spoken a word.

"Yves, get three or four men to help move this man. We need a litter. Get one to bring my bandage case from the clinic. Make them hurry!"

"What happened to him?" she asked the stranger, hardly pausing for breath.

"Boar gash in the thigh," he answered. If he wondered about her credentials, he held his peace. "He lost much blood, and more when I pulled him on my horse." She saw now that he pressed a pad against the wound with one hand—a bunched-up cloak, it looked like. That was well.

"Yves, I need your stool," ordered Gabrielle. Turning again to the horseman, she asked, "Will your horse stay quiet if I approach?"

"He will if I ask him to," he replied, and, oddly, he placed his hand on the horse's neck and murmured to him. Gabrielle had no time to ponder this. She dragged the stool over to the beast's side, stood on it and steadied herself against the broad shoulder.

"I want to have a quick look at the wound, see what we're dealing with," she said, and the stranger nodded. Gabrielle lifted the cloth and saw a deep, ragged puncture, oozing dark blood the minute it was exposed. A vein damaged then, not an artery, or the man would likely already be dead, his heart pumping the blood right out of his body. She clamped the soggy cloth back down and pressed hard, checking the unconscious man's pulse with her other hand.

"Your friend is alive but dangerously weak from loss of blood," she explained. "If we move him off this horse now, it will open the wound and make him bleed more. I'm going to stabilize him right here, seal the cut blood vessel, before we move him. It will take some time, all right?" She glanced up, looking the stranger full in the face for the first time.

He looked ... different. There was nothing she could put her finger on, though he was disconcertingly handsome. Long dark hair, straight brows, luminous gray eyes, a grave manner. Nothing you couldn't find in any local village—well, except maybe those striking eyes. Yet Gabrielle was oddly sure he was not from Verdeau.

He stared at her and his brow cleared. He smiled with a kind of wonderment. "You're a healer." A statement, not a question. "I never hoped to find such a one in a place like this."

The men arrived with bandages and a stretcher, and Gabrielle applied a pressure pad to the gash. Then she braced herself as best she could on the horse's shoulder, placed her hands against the wounded man on either side of the bandage and stilled her mind.

Here was another difference. Usually there was an effort involved in "getting in" to another person's body—a kind of invisible barrier or resistance that had to be felt and eased through. This time, the barrier felt strange, like grasping silk when you were expecting wool. Gabrielle's mind fluttered along its edges as she tried to attune herself to her patient. And then suddenly, effortlessly, she was there, seeing with the inner vision that she alone, of all the people she knew, possessed. She traced the path of the injury, searching for the source of that relentless bleeding. There. The great vein descending from the groin was sliced almost through, but not quite. That was lucky; it meant both ends were still in place. Gabrielle concentrated deeply, summoned the light, channeled and directed it through her hands. It was infinitely more difficult than mending Philippe's shoulder: the boy had been full of life and health, the tissue damage minimal. This man was weakened, the wound lethal and angry, the vein gaping apart. Speed was vital, yet she couldn't rush. The work was painstaking; cell by cell, she had to rejoin the ends of the severed blood vessel, and it had to be strong enough to hold while the injured man was jostled off a horse and onto a stretcher. He hadn't enough blood left to withstand a mistake in judgement.

Time passed, but Gabrielle was unaware of it. She barely seemed alive herself, so motionless and quiet was her trance. The servants with the stretcher shuffled their feet and fidgeted; they knew her reputation and knew better than to disturb her, but inaction in the face of an emergency galled them.

Féolan, however, was almost as still as Gabrielle. He supported Danaïs patiently, though his back and arms began to burn with fatigue. At times his own eyes were closed, his expression one of

deep concentration rather than sleep. Other times he watched
Gabrielle intently, though there was little to see. His horse too
could have been carved in stone. It was only later that onlookers
remarked on how strangely the horse had behaved.

Nearly two hours passed before Gabrielle lifted her head and
looked around, her expression glazed. The world rushed back as
her senses awoke, and she nearly fell off the stool as the cramping
in her calves—she had been standing half on her toes the whole
time—took her by surprise. Yves had to jump forward and help
her down, keeping an arm under her elbow as she stamped her
feet, wincing.

"All right," she said, looking at her waiting helpers. "Thank-you
for waiting. We need to slide this man off the horse and onto the
stretcher. He mustn't be jostled or his leg pulled, or the wound
will re-open. Can—" she broke off, looking up at Féolan. "I'm
sorry, I don't know your name. I am Gabrielle DesChênes, and
this is my father's castle."

"Féolan, of the Elves of Stonewater," he replied. "My companion
is Danaïs. We are deeply in your debt."

A muttering broke out among the men, but Gabrielle merely
gazed at the young man gravely. "You are most welcome here,"
she said, "but I'm afraid further courtesies will have to wait. I
was about to ask, Can you help support your friend off the horse?
Your muscles must be even stiffer than mine."

He smiled ruefully. "They will do anything required, I think,
to move freely again." Still, Gabrielle made sure there was a man
at each of Danaïs' shoulders to take his weight, with the others
supporting his hips and feet. As Danaïs was eased from the horse,
one of the servants cried out.

Gabrielle's attention snapped to his face: "What happened?"

The man mumbled in apology, but his eyes, and those of his fellows, never left Danaïs.

"His ears, m'Lady. I couldn't help myself."

The Elf's blond hair had fallen back from his brow, revealing delicate ears that ended in a subtle but distinct point.

Gabrielle's mouth tightened in disapproval. "We have more important things to worry about right now." A quick check showed the bleeding still under control. "Let's go," she said shortly. The men carrying the litter started off, but Féolan hesitated.

"Our horses . . ."

"Yves will have someone take them to the stables," she replied, slightly irked to see him lingering by the animals instead of staying with his friend. She started after the litter.

Elves, she mused, as she crossed the courtyard for the second time that afternoon. No wonder they seemed different. There were plenty in Verdeau who didn't believe the Elves still lived, at least not in these lands. Even some who argued they were nothing but a fanciful legend, like dragons and unicorns.

Can you call an Elf a "man"? she wondered idly as she headed into the castle.

CHAPTER 2

FÉOLAN watched Gabrielle settle Danaïs into bed, helping where he could. His friend was not yet out of danger, he knew. Danaïs had not regained consciousness, and his face had the yellowish cast of old parchment. And the wound still gaped; it would have to be cleaned and tightly bound.

Gabrielle went about these tasks with a quiet confidence. It was clear that she was trained as well as gifted—well versed in herb-lore too, judging from the rows of neatly labeled jars on her shelves. Féolan held bandages, passed scissors and carried wash-bowls as Gabrielle went to work. For the moment, his confused questions about this mysterious woman would have to wait. He longed to ask how she had come by her ability. No Human he had ever met, and Féolan had walked more among men than most of his kin, had the gift of hand-healing. He had thought it a uniquely Elvish skill. Féolan's thoughts were broken by the clatter of hurried footsteps. The door burst open.

"Hey, Gabi! What's this I hear about—?" The young man stopped abruptly as he took in the guest at his sister's elbow and the gravity of the wounded man's condition.

"I'm sorry," he said, lowering his voice. "I didn't mean to disturb…"

"It's all right, Tris," Gabrielle said with a smile. "Our patient can't hear your booming voice at the moment, and I'm glad you've come. Féolan, this is my brother, Tristan." The two men shook hands. Tristan was not long over the threshold of adulthood, Féolan guessed, though Human age was still hard for him to judge, and with his unruly thick blond hair, boyish energy and friendly grin Tristan might have looked younger than he was.

"Féolan came to us for help when his friend here was attacked by a boar," Gabrielle said. "They'll have to stay for a while. When you have a chance, can you have a room made up? And I haven't had time to be a proper host. Could you introduce him to Father and Mother and make sure an extra place will be set for dinner..."

"Please, I don't wish to be any trouble," Féolan said.

"Nonsense," said Tristan. "No guest of Castle DesChênes ever went short of comfort. Right, Gabi?"

But Gabrielle's attention had turned back to her patient. "Why don't you two go now," she suggested, overriding Féolan's protests. "Your friend—Danaïs, is it?—will be fine without you for a little while. I'm sure you'd like a wash and some clean clothes, at least. I need to sit with him now, and work."

Féolan could feel Gabrielle's intense concentration as she bent over Danaïs. She was shutting out the world, and his presence would only be a distraction. Besides—he grimaced as his hand brushed a crust of half-dried blood on his tunic—he was, in truth, filthy. He allowed himself to be ushered out the door.

"You picked the right place for an accident, anyway," Tristan was saying. "Gabi's the best. If anyone can fix up your friend, it's her." In the hallway, Tristan turned to him. "The servants are all abuzz over the mysterious strangers," he said, laughing. "They say you two are Elvish. Is it true?"

Despite his worry about Danaïs, Féolan found himself smiling and talking easily to the engaging young man as he was led through the castle.

GABRIELLE STRETCHED, THEN winced as her neck protested. The room was dim. Outside the summer sky was the deepening purple-blue of late evening. She had pushed herself hard this day, testing the limits of her power and endurance. Only now that she had surfaced did she feel her own exhaustion. Danaïs, she could tell, was stronger, the wound in his leg mending cleanly and well. But her neck! Long hours bent motionless over her patient had left it with a horrible crick.

Gabrielle rubbed the aching muscles gingerly. It was the price she paid for her gift; that, and the fatigue. She was reminded of a favorite saying of her teacher, Marcus: "See to thy own wounds." Well, and so she would, if she could stay awake long enough.

The warm light had barely kindled under her hands when Danaïs stirred on his pillow. She went to the bedside, ready to quiet him if he awoke in a panic. His eyes opened, eyes as remarkable as Féolan's, she noticed. What was it that gave their eyes such depth and brilliance?

Gabrielle smiled at Danaïs. "Hello," she said softly. "It's good to meet you at last, Danaïs. I am Gabrielle.

"You must lie still," she cautioned, as Danaïs struggled to push himself up from the pillow. "You've been badly injured. You will recover, but you should not move that leg."

Danaïs began to speak in a fluid, musical language that was strange to her. Elvish, she supposed. How lovely it sounded.

"I'm sorry, I don't speak Elvish. I hope you can understand me."

He stared at her and shook his head. "But—how can that be?" he said in her language. His words, Gabrielle noticed, bore a stronger accent than Féolan's, but it was the querulous tone that caught her attention. It was the voice of a sick man whose energy is overtaxed.

Disorientation was not a good sign in a patient, but Danaïs did not seem delirious or even fevered. Perhaps the shock of the accident had left him confused.

"This is a Human city," Gabrielle explained. "You are at Castle DesChênes, the royal castle of the kingdom of Verdeau. Your friend brought you to our gates seeking help when you were wounded."

"But you are ... ," he whispered.

"A pretty good bonemender, lucky for you," she assured him. "And you are still weak and must stop talking for now. Can you drink a little?" Gabrielle poured a careful measure from a beaker on the bedstand into a small glass. "This will ease the pain in your leg and help you rest." She sat with him until his limbs relaxed and he drifted into sleep, then she stretched out on one of the clinic beds. She was desperately tired.

A HAND ON her shoulder awakened her. Féolan. She sat up groggily, aware suddenly of how disheveled she must be. She had been in the same clothes—bloodstained clothes, now—since dawn.

"I'm sorry to wake you," he said. "I brought your dinner." He gestured to a covered tray set on the low table against the wall. "Your family seemed to think you might not have eaten all day."

"Thank-you, I guess I haven't." Gods of the air, she felt half-starved. Her quick breakfast, eaten at daybreak before an early ride along the river, seemed years ago. "Have they looked after you properly?"

"More than properly," he assured her. "I have not eaten so well in many long weeks, nor enjoyed such pleasant company. I had not realized that the King of Verdeau himself was our host. How is Danaïs? Has he awakened at all?"

She saw his concern. "He fares well," she said quickly, reaching for the tray. Even covered, it smelled wonderful. "The wound is mending cleanly, and he did awaken earlier and speak to me. The medicine I gave him will make him sleepy, though, and the rest can only do him good." She tucked in, forcing herself not to gobble: venison in a rich gravy with oatmeal biscuit, the first potatoes of the summer crop, new carrots and a goblet of wine, heavily watered. That would be Tristan's doing, she thought; he knew she steered clear of strong drink when she was working.

"I will sit with him, then," said Féolan, "so you can have a proper night's sleep." She began to protest, but a quick gesture of his hand forestalled her.

"Please," said Féolan. "Let me help in this small way. If Danaïs takes a turn for the worse and needs your skill, I will know it. Surely a servant can fetch you, if need be?"

"Actually, if you pull the cord hanging in the corner there, it will ring in my room and wake me."

"Perfect. You can sleep in peace, then."

Gabrielle nodded in agreement. The room took on a comfortable silence, while Gabrielle ate and Féolan watched his friend. An afterthought nagged at her. "How will you know?"

"How will … I'm sorry, what?"

"You said you would know if Danaïs needed me."

"Oh. The same way I know that you are tired out." He smiled. "I will feel it."

She stared at him. He shrugged. "We can feel other people's emotions," he said. "If Danaïs is in pain or ill or frightened, I will catch an echo of those feelings."

Blessed Mother, thought Gabrielle, with a thrill of recognition. She had experienced this herself but only in moments of deepest concentration, in her healing trance. Then the link between her mind and the patient's body was seamless, intimate, and shadows of his feelings would sometimes gust through her as she worked. But here was a man—no, a whole people—who apparently sensed others' feelings as casually as she herself might note the approach of rain.

She longed to ask Féolan more about it, but he was right, what she needed now was a bath and bed. She finished her dinner, and after leaving dosage instructions for Danaïs' medicine, headed for her chamber.

FÉOLAN SAT LONG by his friend's side, holding one hand between his own two. His expression was distant, as if listening to music far away. He was no healer like Gabrielle, but like most of his people he had some ability to lend strength or encouragement to another in need, especially to one he knew and loved. He did so now, letting his friend know even in sleep that a companion walked beside him still. He sat into the night, until the whole castle was quiet with slumber, until he was sure Danaïs rested easily.

Then he prepared to rest himself. He hesitated, looking at the bed Gabrielle had slept in. Would it be considered improper among these people to use it himself? There were no other linens or blankets to be seen in the room. It seemed pointless, even laughable, to simply move the covers and pillow to a different bed—there were four in the little clinic altogether—and after days of sleeping in the bush he was ill-inclined to slump in a chair all night. In the end, he pulled off his boots and slept on the bed, but under the blanket only, leaving both sheets pulled up. He smiled wryly at this awkward attempt at etiquette—an attempt that was probably all wrong and that, in any case, no one would even witness unless he overslept.

As he lay in the dark clinic, his mind idled over the day. He had been sure Danaïs would die. Though he hated to think of it, the memory of the boar charging replayed over and over in his mind, along with the nightmare struggle to staunch the wound and get Danaïs on the horse, for what? To ride aimless over the trails in search of a road, hoping against hope it led to a nearby settlement and a bonemender who could against all expectation ... And the trails had, against all hope, led him straight to Gabrielle. A Human healer.

"Be honest," he corrected himself, summoning to memory the lustrous copper and gold highlights in her dark hair, the warmth of her smile. "A very beautiful Human healer." He fell asleep thinking of the intriguing young woman who had saved his closest friend.

CHAPTER 3

THE next morning Gabrielle found them both awake and talking quietly together in their own language. This time Danaïs smiled when he saw her.

"Lady Gabrielle," he said. "Féolan has told me what you did yesterday. You have saved my life, and if I can ever serve you it will be my honor." Gabrielle thought he delivered this rather formal speech as if he had planned it out ahead of time. Probably he had, she realized. If you have to say something important in a language not your own, you probably do figure it out ahead of time.

She smiled warmly. "You owe me nothing. To be able to do this—it's all the reward I need. But I thank you for your courtesy." She checked for fever, took his pulse and finally looked at the wound itself. Féolan, watching, gasped as the bandage came away.

Danaïs tensed. "Is it bad?"

"Nay, Danaïs," whispered Féolan, looking from the leg to Gabrielle with frank astonishment. "Nay. 'Tis healing wondrously fast."

Gabrielle's long vigil by the bedside had been rewarded. The wound was clean, uninflamed and visibly shallower than yesterday. It was a long, long way from the life-threatening gash Danaïs had arrived with.

"Could you eat some broth, or a little bread, do you think?" asked Gabrielle.

Danaïs grinned. "I think I could eat almost anything!" he replied.

"That's what I like to hear from a patient. I'll have breakfast sent down," said Gabrielle.

"Could you have them send a tray for me too, Gabrielle?" asked Féolan. "You go have breakfast with your family."

KING JEROME WAS lifting a rather large piece of ham to his mouth as Gabrielle entered the room. "So you decided to favor us with your presence at last," he growled, fork suspended in midair. "Your family not worthy of your company anymore, is it?" Blue eyes glared at her from under wiry brows, and Jerome's freckled complexion darkened to angry brick red. This performance had fooled many people, but not Gabrielle.

"Good morning, Father," she replied. "It's good to see you too."

Tristan cackled. "Why don't you give it up, Father? It never works."

Solange, Gabrielle's mother, patted her husband's shoulder. "There, dear. You do look very fierce, you know. Just not to us."

She turned to her daughter. "How is your patient, Gabrielle?" she asked. "We met the other one, Féolan, last night at dinner. He is quite charming. But he said his friend was terribly hurt."

"He's doing fine, I'm glad to say." Gabrielle helped herself to bread and eggs. "Eating breakfast even as we speak, I hope. Oh, and that young lad, Philippe, who fell off the roof, just a dislocated shoulder, after all. Though it's my belief he jumped."

"You saved the leg, then?" asked Jerome. He looked at his daughter with open pride as she nodded. "It's plain amazing, isn't it? I don't know where you come by that gift, girl, but you leave any bonemender I've ever met in the dust."

"It's not a competition, Father," Gabrielle said primly, but she was pleased nonetheless and she let it show.

"And they really are Elves," marveled Solange. Small and dark-haired, with neat, quick gestures, Queen Solange hailed from the north mainland, while Jerome's sandy coloring, big bones and blunt manner all proclaimed his "Islander" ancestry. "I've never met one before, though my parents used to speak of seeing them now and again. I wonder what brought them our way?"

"I intend to find that out today," announced Tristan.

Gabrielle snorted. "Subtle as ever, Tris." She adored her brash younger brother, but their personalities could hardly have been more different.

THAT DAY THEY fell into a kind of rhythm that set the pattern for the days that followed. Féolan stayed through the morning, helping his friend pass the long hours of recovery. When Gabrielle arrived with lunch for them all, he was singing, accompanying himself on a slim instrument he called a lythra, and the sweet lilt of it was so lovely that she could not bring herself to interrupt but stood by the door listening until the soup got cold. Tristan showed up at lunch too and, as Danaïs seemed to be doing well, was permitted to stay. "But no interrogations, Tris. The man needs peace."

By the time they had eaten Danaïs looked tired, and Gabrielle shooed the others away. Tristan was more than happy to comman-deer Féolan. He offered to ride out with him and show him the surrounding estates, and Féolan was pleased to join him. Gabrielle,

meantime, got down to business: first more medicine to relieve the
relentless torment of the wound. Then she bathed Danaïs, changed
his bandages, and while he napped, worked on healing his leg.

Dinner they took in turns, but Féolan would not budge from
Danaïs's side through the long evenings. Gabrielle often joined
them for a couple of hours, talking quietly or listening to them
sing. Though she knew none of the words, the music seemed to
speak directly to her heart.

On the third evening, Danaïs asked after the horses.

"They are well cared for here," Féolan assured him. "And I
check on them daily."

"You seem very attached to your horses," Gabrielle remarked.
She remembered the day of the accident, when Féolan had seen
to the horses even when his friend was near death. She loved her
own horse, but not that much.

"How not?" asked Danaïs. "They are loyal, patient friends, who
give themselves to our needs. We must be friends in return."

"You talk as though they were Human," said Gabrielle, then
laughed at her own words. "Or should I say, Elvish?"

Féolan smiled. "It's true, though. We are careful of our horses
in Human settlements because Humans do not see animals as
we do and sometimes mistreat them. I have seen gentle beasts
beaten with sticks more than once."

Gabrielle could not deny it, remembered her own hot indignant
tears when as a child she had first witnessed such a thing.

"You ride with no reins," Gabrielle said. "How do you do
that?"

Féolan shrugged. "They carry us of their own will, and they
understand what we ask of them. If there is trust between horse
and rider, there is no need to be pulling this way and that."

They understand what we ask. Gabrielle's mind refused to accept the phrase at face value, but in her heart she knew it was the plain truth. She remembered how Féolan had spoken to his horse at the gatehouse and how the horse had stood like a statue for so long.

"You talk to them," she whispered. They nodded. Gabrielle thought of her gray mare, Cloud, and felt unaccountably close to tears. She said no more.

By the fourth day Danaïs was sitting up and gingerly moving the leg. As his body grew stronger, his cheerful personality emerged. So did his love of good conversation. His command of Krylaise, the language of Verdeau, improved hour by hour. Even Tristan, with his limited tolerance for sitting in any one place for long, was happy to take shifts in the sick room when its patient was awake.

AND TRISTAN, TRUE to his word, wasted no time in unearthing information about their guests' travels. At the breakfast table one morning, he reported his findings.

"They are scouts for the Elves. Féolan is the head scout, but I gather they are few in number. He says the Elves have become so isolated, living in little hidden pockets in the northern forests, that without the scouts they wouldn't know what's going on in the larger world."

"A scout," grunted Jerome. "Not much more than a foot soldier, is it? And we seat him at our table like a high nobleman."

Gabrielle winced. The stock her father placed on rank had bothered her ever since she had become a bonemender. Traveling with her teacher, Marcus, to the outlying villages treating commoners and nobles alike had taught her that nobility, and its opposite, could be found among all people.

"I'm not so sure about that," Tris replied. He reached for the teapot. "He seems to know the decision-makers and a lot about their overall strategies, at any rate. He's the person who saw the need for the scouts in the first place and persuaded their leaders, the Council, I think he called it, to establish regular forays." Tris gulped at the scalding tea, wedged most of a slice of bread into his mouth and swallowed just enough to draw air before adding, "He seemed about to say more at that point but stopped himself. Said something about it not being the time. Very intriguing."

"You may find out soon enough, Tristan," said Solange. "Féolan has requested a formal audience with us. He says he has news that could affect the security of the kingdom."

"I've asked the First General and the Head of King's Council to attend," said Jerome. "You two should be there as well. You know him best, and we will need to judge the credibility of this 'news' of his. Ten bells, in the west study. Let's hope it's worth our while."

CHAPTER 4

T RISTAN was right; Féolan knew how to conduct himself at high levels. Ushered into the formal, wood-paneled chamber by a page, Féolan made his greetings with his customary grave courtesy as he was introduced to Jerome's advisors: First General Fortin, a stocky, plain-spoken man whose incisive mind had proved invaluable many times over Jerome's reign; and Head Councilor Poutin, who inclined his head over his long nose with ill-disguised boredom. Féolan appeared completely at ease as he took his seat at the heavy oak table across from four of the most powerful men in Verdeau. His report, however, was brisk and to the point.

"Your Grace, I have already told your son that I am a scout for the Elves of Stonewater. That is true, but it is only part of my role, which you might call in your language First Foreign Ambassador. It is a small role these days, as the Elves have little contact with other people, but it does give me authority to discuss matters of state with foreign powers." Féolan glanced around the table, inviting questions.

Poutin looked stunned, Gabrielle noticed with amusement. Jerome was not overly fond of the pompous head of King's Council, and Gabrielle was sure her father had deliberately failed to mention the identity of their guest. That will keep him quiet for

a bit, she thought. Tristan would also be enjoying Poutin's discomfiture. She was careful not to meet his eye.

What Féolan said next erased all such thoughts from her
head.

"Our last scouting trip began in the Krylian Mountains. I'm
sure you know that in the steppes beyond those mountains live
the *Gref Orisé*, at least, that is our name for them."

"The Greffaires," muttered General Fortin. "Though I doubt
many in Verdeau have heard of them."

"We are closer neighbors, and Elf memory is long," said Féolan.
"The *Gref Orisé* have not crossed into these lands for hundreds
of years, but your histories will record that about four centuries
ago they poured over the mountains in a massive invasion. Only
after many long months of battle were our combined armies able
to repel them. After that war the Elves retreated to the hidden
valleys where we now make our home and turned away from the
affairs of men.

"My news is this: The *Gref Orisé* have a military encampment
on this side of the mountains—one that we discovered, and who
knows how many we did not? Their men are mapping routes and
stocking supply stations." Féolan paused, letting his words sink
in. "I fear you must prepare for war."

No one spoke. Gabrielle felt her features freeze at Féolan's
blunt announcement and saw the same blank shock on the faces
around the table.

It was the general who broke the silence. "This news is very
important, and I thank you for it," he began. "But does this
camp really threaten us? Our lands do not extend into the far
mountains. Even La Maronne stretches only into the foothills.
The fact that the Greffaires travel mountains that are no one's

territory, for an unknown purpose, does not necessarily mean they intend invasion."

The head councilor nodded.

King Jerome did not. "Armies rarely venture beyond their territory for no reason," he said. "Though they could, I suppose, simply be gathering information for defense purposes. Do you have reason to believe otherwise," he asked Féolan, "besides the lessons of history?"

"Unfortunately, I do," replied Féolan. His gray eyes scanned the room, catching each person's gaze. Gabrielle was chilled by their cold resolve. Féolan's graceful beauty had not left him, but from underneath it had emerged a steely strength. She would not wish to meet this man in battle. "We captured two men and interrogated them separately. They both, eventually, told the same story. They admit the *Gref Orisé* are training for war, gathering men and arms all along their side of the Krylian Mountains. Their captains tell them they will sweep through the Basin to the sea.

"I sent two scouts back to inform my Council, before continuing on," added Féolan. "Though we are well hidden, and our lands not especially prized, we may still be under threat. But the Human settlements certainly are." He turned, now, to address King Jerome directly. "Your Grace, you must prepare for war. And you must engage the neighboring kingdoms. If you do not stand together, the entire Basin may fall."

Jerome sat back in his chair and dragged a hand over his face as though to mop his thoughts clear. Gabrielle saw in the familiar gesture a reflection of her own doubts. They could, and no doubt would, prepare their own defenses. But the four small royalties in the Krylian Basin, a squarish territory ringed by the Krylian Mountain range to the north and west, and by the Gray Sea to east and south, was an alliance only in the most casual sense. Gamier, Barilles, La Maronne and her own Verdeau shared the Basin peaceably, traded, intermarried, spoke the same tongue, but never in living memory had they acted decisively together. It would be no easy task to forge an effective military alliance at short notice.

"How much time do you think we have?" It was Tristan, cutting to the heart as usual.

"I haven't enough information to be sure," Féolan said. "If they are not ready by early autumn—and my guess is they won't be, but it's a shaky guess based on the brief observation of one small camp and the dubious testimony of two low-level soldiers—then I believe they'll wait through the winter. Travel is too treacherous in the mountains. And they won't launch in autumn unless they're very confident. For the same reason, a retreat over the mountains in winter would be disastrous. So, with luck you may have until spring." He didn't need to add what everyone in the room knew. An autumn invasion would catch them almost entirely unprepared.

He glanced at Gabrielle, his eyes troubled. "Your port of Blanchette is the best on the coast. I fear Verdeau will be their primary target."

"YOUR DISCUSSION IS INVITED." King Jerome rarely resorted to this traditional phrasing with his closest advisors. In case anyone had missed it, he was signaling the gravity of the situation.

With Féolan dismissed from the meeting, Councilor Poutin found his voice, along with his superior manner.

"Sire, we know nothing of this man, this so-called Elf. He calls himself a scout. To me, that is merely another word for spy. What is to say he is a friend and not an enemy? Perhaps he does merely report honestly on what he has seen. But what if he does not, and his purpose is to assess our strength for some hostile purpose of his own people?"

"Oh, for the—" Tristan half-rose from the table, but Jerome silenced his outburst with an abrupt gesture.

"Tristan, sit down. The question is fair. An honest face may speak dishonest words." Jerome's children often grew weary of his old sayings, but Gabrielle had to admit the wisdom in this one.

"My King." Gabrielle too, followed the formal rules of the King's Council in her address. "Because Féolan's companion, Danaïs, is grievously injured, I have spent more time than anyone with these Elves." Poutin looked sour. No doubt, Gabrielle thought with some sympathy, he wondered how many other mythical beings were visiting Chênier without his knowledge. "I am sure Féolan is sincere. His concern is genuine as is his gratitude. He does not mean us harm."

Jerome sighed. "My instinct is the same, Gabrielle. I believe he can be trusted. Yet I cannot expect to convince the other kingdoms to call their men to arms on the strength of my instinct."

"Then we must confirm Féolan's report," the General said. "If he will tell us where the camp is, I will send scouts of my own. Meantime, Sire, I suggest we begin our own preparations."

GABRIELLE FOUND FÉOLAN in the clinic with Danaïs.

"They will take action?" he asked her.

She nodded. "I'm afraid you won't see much of Tristan for the rest of your stay. He'll be kept busy now."

"What about you?" asked Danaïs.

She forced a smile. "I'm a bonemender, not a military strategist. And my goal for today is to get you out of bed."

Gingerly at first, Danaïs managed the slow, supported walk into the small garden outside the clinic. He sat on the bench with his leg propped up and lifted his face to the sun while Gabrielle explained the next step of his healing.

"It's mostly up to you now, Danaïs. If you want to regain your full strength you have to begin working the leg. Start with walking, a little farther each day. Take if carefully, though. You have to push a little, or the flesh of your leg will stiffen and shorten around the scar. But if you push too hard, you will re-injure yourself."

"Yes, ma'am," Danaïs said humbly, ducking his head and wringing his hands like a downtrodden servant.

"None of your cheek. I'm not joking."

"Yes, ma'am."

The three sat companionably together. The day was flawless, all blue sky and gentle breeze, but in the silence Gabrielle's mind returned to the discussion in the king's chamber. A sense of foreboding crept over her. The scouts would take too long. The alliance would come together too late. And what then?

A hand touched her shoulder, jarring her out of her gloom. "I am sorry to be the bearer of such news," said Féolan.

Gabrielle shrugged. "I wish I could talk with you about it. But we've been told to keep War Council discussions secret." She could hardly believe that Verdeau now had a War Council.

"I'm glad to hear it," he replied. "It means the matter is being taken seriously."

"They will really come?"

"I believe so. But they cannot, now, take the country by surprise. You must trust in your father and his general."

Gabrielle nodded. Her eyes followed the heavy path of a bumble bee as it lumbered from one red bergamot blossom to another, but her mind brooded on the future. With an effort, she turned away from her gloomy thoughts.

"How did you two end up doing this? The scouting, I mean."

"That is Féolan's story," Danaïs said. "I will leave it to him, while I sleep here in the sun."

Féolan thought for a moment. "The beginning is easy enough," he said. "I had a young man's wanderlust, and I did not see why it should be confined to the wildernesses my people love to roam. There was a whole civilization to explore, and I thought, Why do we commune with trees and beasts, but not with Humans? Surely they are at least as interesting."

"Thank-you very much," said Gabrielle, and Danaïs, on the chair beside her, smirked in his "sleep."

"I expressed that badly," Féolan apologized. "But in truth my thoughts at the time were not far ahead of my words. I studied Krylaise and began to visit Human towns on my travels. And I learned that we ignored the world around us at our peril. Pirates were raiding along the coast; an epidemic raged among the Gamier sheep. These things could affect us. Yet at the time, we would not even have known if the Humans became hostile to our settlements. So it was no act of genius to conclude we needed to have Elves—Elves who could speak the language and be at ease among Humans—keeping abreast of Human affairs."

"Yes," Gabrielle nodded. "It seems odd to me that no one had thought of it before." She tried to imagine a Verdeau that never had contact with the neighboring kingdoms of the Basin, and the very idea seemed absurd.

"My people were not always so isolated," said Féolan, "but most now are content, it seems, to live in their own secluded world. For some reason, I am not."

"Ah, and that's the real question," Danaïs chimed in. "Why does Féolan, who could be settling down, taking on some responsible position which would groom him for a place on Council—it's true, Féolan, with your parentage you would have only to stay out of trouble and it would be yours—instead choose to head up the scouts? For the rest of us, it is only an occasional duty, a chance to travel and learn, and then go home. He is away as often as not."

Gabrielle gazed at Féolan. There were bonemenders, she knew, who lived thus, traveling ever from village to village. It seemed a rootless kind of life.

His smile seemed a little embarrassed. "Danaïs makes me sound like a vagabond. It's not that I dislike my home. I suppose … well, I've come to feel that Humans have a lot to teach us."

"Such as?" Gabrielle asked. She wasn't teasing; she honestly wanted to know what these people, with their extraordinary abilities, could learn from her kind.

"Humans are more … direct? That's not quite right." Gabrielle could almost see Féolan trying on words and was reminded that Krylaise was not his first tongue. "They have an energy, a fierceness almost, in the way they live. Some endure such hardship, but they strive still for life, however brief. Maybe it's a kind of courage." He shrugged, defeated. "I guess I don't really know. But I find I like to be around it."

Danaïs snorted, eyes still closed. "You can see his years of study have led to a deep understanding of Humankind."

But Gabrielle smiled at Féolan, her heart warmed by his words. "I see the courage you speak of in the people I treat. I met a woman once whose husband had died. She was working a farm and raising six children alone, and the youngest was so crippled he could not walk. And she was tireless in her care and protection of that child. She humbled me."

"Yes," said Féolan.

He held her gaze, and Gabrielle felt a sudden connection, a flow of understanding that went beyond words. Danaïs and the little garden faded away for a moment, as though she and Féolan spoke in some private place. Flustered, Gabrielle pulled her eyes back to the bergamot patch, staring at the tangled plants as though she planned to count each blossom.

In the silence that followed, Féolan gave a dramatic sigh. She looked up and caught his amused grin.

"What is it?" she asked, glad to lighten the mood.

"That Poutin fellow. I fear we shall never be soul-brothers."

CHAPTER 5

DESPITE Gabrielle's feeling that her world had changed overnight, life continued much the same as ever. She was aware that meetings were being held, envoys sent, but for her there was the usual trickle of patients to care for, Danaïs' leg to finish healing, FirstHarvest Feast to plan with her mother … and medicines to prepare. This last she came close to forgetting. It was with a start she realized the hawkweed had come into bloom and the moon was almost full.

"You will have to do your exercises by yourself tomorrow," she told Danaïs that afternoon. She had added stretching and strength work to his daily walks. She patted his head as though he were a small boy and put on a sugary sweet voice. "I'm sure you'll do your very best."

"Yes, ma'am."

"Féolan here will come and glare at you sternly to make sure you don't skimp."

"Yes, ma'am. Where are you going to be, ma'am, if I might ask?"

"I need to gather some herbs, especially the hawkweed flowers, which are strongest when they first bloom. I was taught it's best to gather on a waxing moon. I'm not really sure there's any truth to it, but I like to honor the old traditions."

Danaïs dropped the humble patient pose. "Why don't you take Féolan along? He's a lazy sot, not much use really, but at least one of the horses would get exercised."

"Yes, of course." It was nice of Danaïs to make the suggestion for her. "Féolan, if you'd like to, you're most welcome. I'm going to ride into the upland pastures east of here."

IT WAS A PLEASANT RIDE, first through the southern tip of the town of Chênier, which sprawled in a rough semi-circle at the castle's feet and crowded up against the Avine River's eastern bank, and then east along a country track through open farmland. Gradually the orchards and ploughed fields gave way to rougher, hilly country, scrubby woodlots and livestock pasturage. Gabrielle turned off the track and headed up a farm lane.

They met the farmer himself repairing a break in the fencing. Squinting up at them, he scrambled to his feet and managed an awkward bow.

"Hello, Luc. How's your family?"

"Very well, I thank ye, m'Lady. Come for the hawkweed and that, have ye?"

"Yes, if it's still all right with you. Is it thick in that back pasture again this year?"

"Whole field's orange with 'em. You're more'n welcome."

Thanking the man, Gabrielle turned her horse and led Féolan past the farmhouse and through a series of fields, until they reached an untrimmed pasture snugged up against a strip of woodland. Sure enough, the hawkweed glowed orange and golden in the sun.

They worked side by side for about an hour, snapping off the flower heads and packing them into Gabrielle's big gathering bags.

Later she would dry and grind them. The flowers eased inflammation and fever and were mildly sedating, and Gabrielle used them both as a poultice for wounds or sprains and in medicinal teas.

As the two bags filled up, Féolan turned to Gabrielle.

"How much do you need?"

Her face darkened. "I don't know. Normally I just take the one bag. This year, though ... maybe we'll need a lot more."

They filled a third bag together and stopped for a break. Gabrielle had packed ale and cheese and strawberry pie, and she stretched out on a smooth, sunny outcropping of rock and savored the rich fruit. "That's the taste of summer," she sighed.

As they ate, Féolan asked, "How did you learn your craft? You have a rare gift."

"I suppose I do," Gabrielle replied. "I have never met another who could do it. But then, I have only met three or four bone-menders in my life, and there are many more than that. I see no reason to assume I am unique."

"Did someone teach you the hand-healing?"

"I discovered it quite by accident," Gabrielle laughed. "I fell off my horse when I was fourteen, landed on a rock and cut my knee pretty badly. The blood scared me a little. I clapped my hands over the cut, wanting to cover it from sight. But then I felt something start to happen in my hands. And even though it was so strange, it didn't feel frightening. It felt right. So I just let it happen. And my knee stopped bleeding.

"I didn't dare tell anyone at first. And it didn't occur to me it would work on another person until over a year later, when one of our sheep dogs was savaged by a wolf." Gabrielle remembered it vividly. The poor dog had dragged himself home, barely able to walk, and fallen in a bloody heap.

"He was all ripped up, and Jacques, the kennel master, was going to kill him. Oh, it broke my heart, such a brave, loyal dog he was. I knelt beside him and stroked him, and I felt it in my hands again—you know, they feel warm and bright and sort of tingly as the healing flows through them. My heart started just hammering in my chest at the thought."

"And you saved him?" said Féolan.

"Yes. The hardest part was getting rid of Jacques. Imagine this haughty stripling of a girl, staring him down and ordering him off. The poor man turned nearly purple and stormed out. I was sure he was off to fetch my mother and have me dragged home."

Féolan snorted, and Gabrielle grinned. "I know, it wasn't very diplomatic of me. But I was frantic."

"You must have caused quite a stir when you healed that dog."

"Well I didn't totally heal him, of course. I didn't know how to stitch or dress a wound. Even now it takes ages to seal a wound fully the other way. But I did stop the bleeding, and I managed to perk him up considerably. When Jacques came back, a long time later, the dog looked more alive than dead, rather than the other way around. He took one look, sort of hissed between his teeth and disappeared. A minute later he was back with an armful of bandages. And I was so worn out I keeled over and fell asleep in the straw beside them."

"How did your parents react?"

"Oh, they were wonderful," said Gabrielle. "Well, eventually. Not at first. At first they didn't believe it. They thought I must have tricked the kennel master somehow, though they could hardly believe that either. Practical jokes weren't exactly my style.

"There was some shouting from my father and tearful protests from me, and finally I grabbed a kitchen knife and cut my arm and proved what I could do. Rather melodramatic, I'm afraid. There was dead silence then. My mother burst into tears, and so did I, and when everyone calmed down I told them I wanted to study to be a bonemender. I couldn't have such a gift and not use it. They agreed. The day after my sixteenth birthday, I started my apprenticeship with the Chênier bonemender."

Old Marcus had not been eager to accept her, Gabrielle recalled. He had taken her, in the end, only because his king and queen had requested it, expecting to be saddled with a spoiled princess indulging a passing whim. In the first weeks her teacher had taken pains to strip away any glamorous notions she might have held: Gabrielle had scrubbed bedpans, vomit, soiled bedsheets and the clinic itself, ground herbs until her arms ached and healed not a single person. After three months, Marcus had acknowledged that she was serious; he soon discovered she was also quick to learn, and the years of her apprenticeship had been deeply rewarding for both of them.

Gabrielle shook herself out of her reverie. Marcus, and the other bonemenders too, should be alerted to the coming danger. Probably the whole country should be stockpiling extra bandaging and herbs. She would speak to her father about it.

"I'd better get back to work. I want to harvest the comfrey while we're here," said Gabrielle. "It grows all over these hills. This is dirtier work, I'm afraid." If there was war, then this herb, known for its virtue in helping bones knit and wounded flesh regenerate, would be essential. For this she needed the whole plant, roots and all. Féolan helped her dig the hairy, rambling plants from the stony ground.

"I know this one," he exclaimed. "It grows in our woodland too. We call it, oh, I guess it might translate into 'knitbone'."

"Some people call it 'ass ear'," she said, smiling as she stroked the fuzzy leaf. "But knitbone is a very good name."

As they worked, Féolan told Gabrielle about the Elvish healers and what he knew of their techniques and medicines. The time passed quickly, and as they rode home the late afternoon sun slanted over the fields, illuminating each blade of grass. The sight set Féolan to daydreaming about Gabrielle's eyes: a softer green, they were, but with that same impression of golden light under the surface.

CHAPTER 6

IRST Harvest drew near. Festivities were planned throughout the country for the high summer festival celebrating the early crops' bounty, but in Chênier the biggest event was the King's Feast. The castle hall would be especially crowded this year. Jerome had "invited" the territorial regents and garrison commanders, taking advantage of the opportunity to hold a full tactical meeting without causing undue alarm.

Gabrielle and Solange had been working with the household staff for days to prepare for FirstHarvest Feast. Feeding well over a hundred people lavishly was no simple task, especially in high summer when food spoiled quickly in the heat. Whatever could be done ahead of time was, but when the day arrived, the cooks would still have to start before dawn.

Now it was late afternoon, and Gabrielle was dressing in her chamber. From a young age she had been trained to be a gracious host, sitting at high table with her parents at all the feasts and festivals that marked the cycle of their life, and despite her natural shyness she enjoyed these duties. In the small kingdoms of the Krylian Basin, the royal families were not distant, awesome figures but practical leaders. Their participation in festivals and other public events was expected, not that they hid themselves away at other times. Even Gabrielle's work as a healer, though it stretched the boundaries of custom, was not considered unseemly. Kings and queens were meant to care for their people. Gabrielle's gift was Verdeau's good fortune, and only strengthened the people's loyalty to the Crown. But medical emergencies aside, she was still a royal daughter, with all the demands and formalities that entailed. Tonight Féolan and Danaïs would be their guests, and Gabrielle was looking forward to that too.

She dressed with care, aware that she wanted to look attractive. Standing in front of the glass, she eyed herself critically. The simple dark green dress she had chosen set off her chestnut hair and fitted her willowy figure perfectly. She wondered now, though, if it was too plain, and whether she should have chosen a more elaborate hairstyle. She had had her maid braid the sides and fasten them with a jeweled clasp at the back but allowed the rest to fall in natural waves down her back.

She sighed. It was unlike her to fret over her appearance. Who are you trying to impress? she asked herself peevishly.

Like it's not obvious, a sly voice whispered in her mind. A teasing girlfriend's voice it was, and just as relentless. Like you haven't noticed him.

Gabrielle gazed at herself, startled. Was she attracted to Féolan? She had to laugh at her own huffy mental protests: I enjoy his company, that's all. I'm interested in his abilities.

Oh yes, his abilities, mocked the girlfriend's voice. And his eyes. And his smile. And that feeling you get when he talks to you alone. And...

Enough. At twenty-seven, she was well past the usual age of marriage, resigned to a single life. It had been years now since she had considered any man as a potential mate.

Strange how that had happened. She had certainly had suitors once she came of age at seventeen; she was, after all, the daughter of a king, and no one had ever called her ugly. Her days had been dominated by her training with Marcus, but still she had gone with the hopeful young men for walks and horseback rides, chatted through dinners and teas and games of four-spot or chiggers. There had been visits to her father's people on Crow Island and to her mother's people in the interior and even to the neighboring kingdoms of Gamier and Barilles. At twenty she became a qualified bonemender with no serious prospects of marriage, though everyone was careful to add "yet." By the time she turned twenty-two, the suitors had stopped calling.

It was her own fault, if fault could be laid for such a thing. She just hadn't been interested, not in any of them. She had let the ones she liked best kiss her, hoping to feel the stirring of desire the troubadours sang about. But she hadn't. One by one, the young men, and a couple of older ones, had drifted away, puzzled and discouraged. There had been only one marriage proposal, from a widowed Barilles nobleman, and though he tried to hide it she knew he had been relieved by her polite refusal. There was something in Gabrielle too, despite her gentle manner, that men found forbidding.

She had been surprised, and grateful, that her parents had not pushed her to marry, though Solange had given at least one speech about how married couples "grow into love." They might have been less accepting, Gabrielle thought wryly, if her older brother, Dominic, had not already produced an heir.

Since there were no men Gabrielle wanted, it had been easy enough to give up on marriage. Much, much harder was giving up the hope of children. Running like a secret rising tide of panic through her youth had been the growing fear that she was barren. As it turned out, the problem was nothing more than a dramatically late puberty. But who would ever have believed it could be so late? On the night of her eighteenth birthday Gabrielle had wept until dawn, sure that if she had not started her moon cycles by now she never would. She carried the sorrow alone, unable to bring herself to confide even in Solange. Almost a year later, her cycles had started. Not that they had been much use, after all.

And now here she was, trying on jewelry and worrying about her hair. Wanting, why not admit it, Féolan to find her pretty.

She couldn't decide if she liked the feeling or not. It doesn't matter anyway, she chided herself. It's just a dinner, and he'll be gone in a few days. Fastening the silver clasp at her waist, she strode out of the room.

FÉOLAN AND DANAÏS HAD also dressed with care, if less indecision. Their choice was simple: the travelworn clothes they had been living in for weeks, or the one good outfit each had stuffed at the bottom of his pack. As guests at an occasion of some importance, they knew they should look the part. With the help of a young maid, who had steamed the wrinkles out of tunics and cloaks, they were presentable enough.

Féolan knocked on Danaïs' door. "Ready to go?"

"In a minute," came the muffled reply. "I just have to get this miserable boot on."

Féolan knew better than to offer his help. Just last night, Danaïs had been declared no longer a patient and moved into a proper guest room. Féolan suspected Gabrielle had done it to enforce a new exercise regime: now Danaïs would have to labor up and down the curving oak stairway several times a day. Danaïs, however, had been extremely pleased, and with his private quarters had come a determined return to independence.

Soon Danaïs emerged, and Féolan did help him with the stairs. They walked down the corridor, opened the double doors to the Great Hall and entered a scene of genial pandemonium. The massive room had been transformed; rows of tables and benches filled the formerly empty space while a dozen overhead chandeliers flickered with candlelight and reflected off the glass goblets set at each table.

Nobody was seated, though most of the guests had arrived. The Great Hall was congested with people, clumped along the edges of the room or threading their way between tables to shake hands and slap backs. The hubbub of conversation was punctuated with frequent shrills of laughter; Féolan thought it likely that a good number of the guests had kicked off the feast, at least the drinking part of it, before leaving their homes. He caught site of Tristan's blond hair by the far entrance; Tristan appeared to know everybody there and was making a brave attempt at greeting them all. Féolan scanned the room and picked out Jerome and Solange in another corner, smiling and welcoming the guests. There was method underlying this apparent madness, then. And—

Féolan's breath caught in his throat as he found Gabrielle's slender form. The candlelight flickered over her dark hair, making it flash red and gold when she turned her head. Her eyes looked deeply green, nearly as dark as her dress. Gabrielle was on duty too, her style quieter than Tristan's but just as effective as she gave each person in turn her warm attention. She was talking now to a couple with a babe in arms, exclaiming over the child, laughing as it reached for her silver earring.

Féolan stood quietly, watching the scene. He wasn't at all sure Danaïs should risk making his way into that jostling crowd. A sudden horn fanfare saved him the worry as people headed for the tables.

"Féolan! Danaïs! Over here!" Tristan appeared before them and pointed toward a dais at the near end of the room, where a white-draped, richly set table was flanked with banks of flowers. "Come, you'll sit up top with us." Tris looked them up and down, gave a slow whistle. "Ver-ry nice. Very dashing. You'll have the seamstresses going crazy, every young nobleman demanding an Elvish cloak and brow-gem."

Jerome and Solange were already at table, standing at their places. Beside Jerome stood a dark-haired man, a woman and two children. "My older brother, Dominic, and his family," explained Tristan. "He is regent of Crow Island and the Blanch-ette coast."

Gabrielle soon joined them. Her eyes widened as she took in the Elves' finery.

"My Lord Danaïs, my Lord Féolan," she murmured, dropping them an elegant curtsy.

Féolan returned his best Human bow, then placed his hand over his heart. "Among my people we do thus, then touch palms," he explained, and smiling up at him, she followed suit.

Tristan and Gabrielle took their places beside Solange, and Féolan and Danaïs were seated on their left. That left one empty place on their side of the table, and this was soon taken by an older woman introduced as the Regent of Inner Verdeau.

"My aunt Marisse," Gabrielle muttered in his ear.

Further introductions were abandoned as the king stepped to the front of the dais. The room quieted. Jerome's speech was brief but masterfully delivered: a warm welcome, a vote of appreciation to the laborers and landowners responsible for the harvest, a prayer for continued good bounty and the promise of after-dinner entertainment. As he settled himself at the table, servants began bringing in food, and the guests cut short their applause in a hasty dive for their seats.

Dinner passed in a blur of rich food, flowing ale and increasingly loud talk. Marisse proved as gracious as her sister, Solange, and accepted the Elves with matter-of-fact warmth, a welcome change from the incredulity they had become used to. "How wonderful to meet you," she had exclaimed. "In the interior, you know, we still speak of a time when Elves and Humans were allies. Perhaps those days will come again."

"Perhaps they will," Féolan replied, privately picturing the disaster that might force just such an alliance.

A ripple of amusement from Danaïs and Gabrielle chased away this unpleasant train of thought, amusement at Tristan's expense, it turned out. Tristan had been restlessly scanning the crowded room since the meal had started. Now he had evidently found what he was searching for. He had aimed that charming grin of his right across the Great Hall, and it was all but giving off sparks. That smile's for a woman, Féolan thought, and a second later Tristan proved him right by blowing a kiss out into the air.

Gabrielle shot him a quick elbow in the ribs. "Tris, behave."

"What?!" protested Tristan, all indignity and wounded innocence. "What'd I do?"

Danaïs' carefully neutral expression crumpled into a chuckle. "You nearly set my ear on fire with that kiss. I felt my skin sizzle as it flew past me!" he said. Their laughter was lost in the clatter of dishes that announced the arrival of the next course.

"Poor Rosalie," sighed Gabrielle, still giggling. "If she only knew what she was getting into with—" An unladylike squawk startled their end of the table; Tristan had reached behind and yanked her hair. Gabrielle looked at the guests apologetically, her eyes merry. "I am sorry. You know even now, my brother and I still can't be trusted to sit together."

AS THE LAST PLATES were cleared away, the room turned expectantly toward the empty end of the dais where the musicians would play. Applause swelled through the audience as the five musicians trooped onstage.

They knew how to please a large crowd, playing and singing with gusto and sticking to the rollicking shanties and drinking songs that could be enjoyed without really listening. Féolan found Human music rather crude, but he had come to appreciate its energy and momentum, and he enjoyed the concert. He had even learned a few of the songs in his travels and impressed Tristan hugely by joining in on the sing-along choruses. Gabrielle sang along too, her voice a clear contralto.

After about an hour, Jerome stepped forward and deftly ended the party. Everyone stood, as well as they could manage, for the Verdeau anthem, and then the entire head table was ushered out of the room, followed by the musicians.

"No more wine, no more music. They'll all clear out soon enough," Jerome assured his wife. He turned to his assembled guests. "Good night, everyone. Those of you who are here for business as well as pleasure, we meet at nine bells in the Council Chamber."

Most people headed for the stairs, but Tristan held the two Elves back. "The musicians will play a little more for us in the salon. Would you like to come?"

Of course they would. Tristan disappeared for a moment and returned with Rosalie in tow, a short, dark-haired young woman with huge brown eyes. Dominic stayed as well: "Mother made me come as a chaperone, to make sure Tristan doesn't disgrace himself!"

GABRIELLE HAD PLACED herself behind Danaïs, Féolan noticed. She was watching her patient walk. He dropped back himself and tried to observe Danaïs with a healer's eyes. There was a stiffness to his gait but no obvious limp, which seemed pretty good for such a recent injury and after a long day. Féolan glanced at Gabrielle, who nodded—it was pretty good.

Gabrielle gave the musicians a warm welcome; Tristan, for his part, wasted no time in pouring them a round of wine. Then he threw himself on a settee and pulled Rosalie down beside him. When the others were settled, the musicians began an instrumental piece that was unlike anything Féolan had yet heard at the taverns and inns where he had stayed. It began quietly, just the whistle and mandola delicately intertwined. Gradually the other instruments joined in, trading melody and countermelody in a complex weaving until finally all five came together in a single, stirring voice. Féolan realized that he had far underestimated the troupe's skill.

Gabrielle, he could tell, found a sweet, simple happiness in the music. Her shining eyes were glued to the troupe as they played on, an old ballad about a sea battle, then a pretty country love song. Then the leader motioned to Tristan. "Lord Tristan, come up and sing with your sister. Does your famous duet have anything new for us?"

Tristan stepped forward, motioning to Gabrielle. "Nothing new, this time. We've been unaccountably busy, I'm afraid. But we'll gladly subject you to the same old thing, won't we Gabi?"

Gabrielle hesitated, but when Dominic pleaded, "Come on, Gabrielle, I haven't heard you sing in so long," she gave a quick nod and stood up. Glancing at Féolan, she colored a little, and he realized with chagrin that she would feel freer without him there.

It didn't matter. Once she began, all embarrassment seemed to drop away. She and Tristan sang "Tables Turned," a rollicking off-color song about a husband who has been untrue during his long travels. Trading verses full of lame excuses and double entendres, Gabrielle and Tristan sang it with exaggerated broad humor. Rosalie, who had never heard it before, collapsed in laughter at Gabrielle's "last word":

I've ridden up, I've ridden down
Deep vale and highest hill
I've ridden farther even than thee
So travel where you will.

WITH A SWEEPING BOW, Tristan returned to his seat, but the harpist said, "Stay, Lady Gabrielle, and sing something pretty. Sing that shipwreck song."

Féolan expected some brave account of a lost crew. What he heard, instead, was a woman's lament for her love, drowned at sea and washed up on a foreign shore among strangers. The

melody was simple and lovely, the lyrics poignant with under-
stated grief:

Pity the hearts
The wild waves part...
For my love is far, far away.

But it was Gabrielle's voice that made the hairs on his
neck stand on end: lower than an Elvish voice, it had nearly
the same liquid clarity, with a rich emotional resonance he
had not heard among his own people. Never melodramatic,
Gabrielle's singing nonetheless evoked fear and loneliness, love
and courage. Féolan thought he could listen to her forever.

As Gabrielle stepped down, someone asked the Elves for a song.
They stopped at one, knowing that most people have a limited
appetite for lyrics in a foreign tongue. Not much later, Dominic
rose. "I'm charged with keeping Tristan and myself clearheaded
for tomorrow's meetings," he said. "I think we'd better call it a
night."

Working their way up the stairs—Danaïs' leg was complaining
now, and they fell behind the others—the two Elves marveled
once again at Gabrielle's mysterious talents. "We have misjudged
them, the Humans, based only on the few we have met," suggested
Féolan. "I did not think to find a healer's hands among them, nor
for that matter such fine musicianship. I did not expect them to
vary so, one from another."

"Aye, perhaps," said Danaïs. "But you could meet the whole city,
I warrant, and that maid would still stand out like the brightest
star in the sky."

Féolan nodded his agreement, but he did not go on to confess
the fear that kept him awake until dawn: that against all wisdom,
he had fallen in love with a Human.

CHAPTER 7

"HOW soon will I be ready to travel?"

Gabrielle had just finished checking Danaïs' leg. She had expected the question, of course; Danaïs spoke often of his family, and it was clear that he was eager to get back to them. But she hadn't expected the question to give her a painful knot in her throat. It was hard to think of saying good-bye.

She swallowed, found her voice and hoped it would come out steady. "Very soon, I'd say, especially if you're willing to take it slow at first. But you should ride your horse a few times before you go, maybe a couple of short rides around the grounds today, building up to a good long ramble. It's a whole different use of your leg muscles."

And so it was that, two days later, they headed on horseback into the hills for a picnic lunch. Tristan had managed to join Gabrielle and the Elves, and, though it was not said aloud, everyone knew it was their farewell ride.

Gabrielle was grateful for Tristan's presence; his buoyant spirits kept her own sadness at bay. He mimicked the Elves' reinless riding and nearly fell off his horse when it suddenly began to trot. He taught Féolan and Danaïs a popular drinking song, and they climbed up the trail serenading the wildlife in four-part harmony.

They spread out a blanket on a sunny, open hillside and while Danaïs eased out the cricks in his leg, Gabrielle set out the meal: cold chicken, fresh bread, tiny new cucumbers and carrots, the summer's first raspberries and oatmeal cake.

"Nothing to drink?" demanded Tristan.

"Sorry, I forgot." Gabrielle tried hard to look penitent. She watched Tristan's face fall before she added, "Of course you could check the saddlebags ... " He returned from Cloud triumphant, a bottle of ale in one hand and apple cider in the other.

The food and drink slowly disappeared, and the noon sun beat down on their heads. In the drowsy heat, the buzzing of the first cicadas rose in its loud drone and fell away. First Tristan, then Danaïs, lay back, tipped their hats over their faces and slept.

Gabrielle had had good reason to suggest this particular hillside. She motioned to Féolan. "Over there, where the woods begin, I found mandragora last year. I'm going to check if it's still growing there."

"I'll help you," said Féolan quickly, scrambling to his feet. "Mandragora ... is that the plant with the big shiny leaf and the root that looks like a little man?"

"That's the one."

"*Mandrakas.* I've heard it's a poison."

"It is. It's very dangerous to use. I hate it. But it's the only thing I know that will make a person sleep insensibly. If there's a war ..." Féolan saw what she was picturing: amputations, burns, disembowelments. There was no need to say more.

"Should we tell someone we're going?" he said, as much to change the subject as anything else.

"Tris will figure it out," she said with a smile. "I have a habit of doing this."

After some casting around, Gabrielle found the mandragora patch just a short distance into the wood. They loosened the plants with the little digging tools she had brought, careful not to break, bruise or even rub against any part, and laid them on the double thickness of muslin Gabrielle had spread on the ground. When they were finished, she would wrap the plants securely before packing them into her bag.

"Danaïs is almost recovered," said Gabrielle. "You'll be leaving soon." A painfully obvious statement, addressed to the uprooted mandragora plants laid out beside her. She didn't know why she had even said it. Her face hot with embarrassment and suppressed sadness, she kept her eyes glued to her work.

"Yes," Féolan replied. He loosened the last threads holding his plant. Tugged it free. Leaned over and laid it on the muslin, his shoulder nearly touching hers. Took a breath. "I've been meaning to ask you…" He paused again. "Gabrielle, I was wondering…Would you consider coming back with us for a time? I know our healers would want to learn about your abilities and would be glad to share their knowledge with you. And I could bring you home well before winter."

This was unexpected. "Oh, I've never met another…It's a tempting thought," she confessed. And it was. After so many years of feeling her way alone, to meet someone who understood this type of healing, who could teach her…She felt a stir of excitement, the call of her work. It was a wonderful opportunity. And yet she had hoped for something different, hadn't she? Something more personal. She hid her disappointment.

"I will think on it, Féolan. Thank-you for inviting me."

"Gabrielle."

She felt Féolan's intensity, glanced up and met his eyes. Luminous gray, like rain, like an ocean shot with sunshine. He held her gaze.

"I have my own reasons for asking you to return with me. My heart is strongly drawn to you. If it is not a fool's hope that you share my feelings, I would love the chance to know you better."

His fingers curled around her hand and lifted it. His lips brushed her knuckles.

She did not know that her whole body leaned toward that kiss. She only knew that she was suddenly in his arms, that to be held by him was like water in the desert. His hands were in her hair, his breath against her cheek. Then he kissed her, and she learned that the poets were right, after all.

It was a long time before he drew back. "I don't know much about the love customs of Humans," Féolan admitted, "but my diplomat's training is warning me to slow down."

Gabrielle nestled into the curve of his arm as they sat together. She was too full of her own happiness to notice the troubled undertone in Féolan's mood. He rested his cheek against her hair, tightened his arms around her and sighed.

"Of all the dangers I thought to face in my travels among the Humans, falling in love was not one of them," he confessed. It seemed a joke, but his voice was serious.

"Why danger?" Gabrielle asked. "Is it forbidden among your people?" Was there some anatomic difference that would cause difficulty? she wondered uneasily. Apart from the ears, she hadn't noticed anything remarkable about Danaïs.

"No, not forbidden. Discouraged, rather. There are old stories and songs about love between Humans and Elves, of course. Mostly cautionary tales."

"But why?" she asked again, turning her head to peer into his face.

"Well," he said. He didn't like to talk about it, that much was clear. "Because, you know, of the difference in life spans."

"I don't know, Féolan," she flared. "I don't know anything about your people. Tell me."

He swallowed. "I'm sorry, Gabrielle. I thought you would know. I guess I forgot how long it's been that Elves have kept apart from men."

He spoke gently now. "You see, we live a lot longer than you do. So an Elf who falls in love with a Human is doomed to lose her."

"How much longer?" she asked bluntly. "How long will you live?"

"Five, maybe six hundred years."

Gabrielle's face went blank. "Five …," she whispered. A roaring in her head made it impossible to think. Then the horror of it rose in her as she saw the inevitable course of lives so hopelessly mismatched. She thought she might be sick. A kind of rage swept through her. She struggled to her feet.

"Five hundred years!" she shouted. "Are you mad? How can you speak to me of love? To touch me like that!" She turned and ran.

Blundering through thick brush, thinking only to be safely out of earshot, Gabrielle finally sank against a huge, gray, beech trunk. Only now, in her bitterness, did she know how deeply she had wanted this man.

She had been given a last chance at love, only to have it shrivel and die in her hand. Drawing up her knees, she buried her face in her arms and sobbed.

"GABRIELLE."

Feolan sat silently beside her, as though trying to gain the trust of a wounded animal. She had only gradually become aware of him, and she was too worn out to send him away. She just stayed there, curled into her own arms, pretending he wasn't there. He hadn't moved either, not until her tears had run dry.

Now he had spoken, and there was no more pretending. She lifted weary, red-rimmed eyes to his. "Féolan, please."

"Gabi, I'm so sorry to have hurt you." He had never called her that. No one but Tristan had ever called her that. "But I don't understand. I know this is a shock, but is it so impossible?"

"Of course it's impossible."

"But why? I mean, why for you? We could still have a lifetime together—one of your lifetimes. How is that different from what you would have with another Human?"

Gabrielle stared at him. He didn't see it. She had told him to spell things out for her. Now she would have to do the same.

"Féolan, think about it. I will not be like I am now until the day I die. I am twenty-seven years old. In thirty years I'll be gray and stiff in the joints. For the last twenty years of my life I'll be a wrinkled, bent, frail old woman, and you will be in the full flush of youth. You won't be my lover—you'll be my nursemaid."

Féolan bowed his head. He sat in silence for a long while, and when he looked up, he did not hide the wetness on his cheeks.

"Yet would I walk with you to the end, if you would have me."

Mother goddess, help me, thought Gabrielle wildly. A fist clenched her heart.

"No, Féolan," she finally managed. "It would turn to bitterness. Better to stop now." It came to her that these might be their last private words, and she reached for the strength to speak her heart.

"But I would take back my angry words. When I am old and on my deathbed, I will remember that once a shining Elf-lord loved me, and that will bring me joy."

Féolan hitched a deep breath, nodded, wiped his face with the back of his hand. He tried to smile. "The others will be wondering if we've been attacked by a boar."

"Will you make some excuse for me? I need to be alone for a while. I'll make my own way back."

Féolan reached out and took a lock of her hair between his fingers. Sliding his hand down its length, he brought it to his lips and kissed it. Then he was gone.

CHAPTER 8

GABRIELLE spent the next two days as far away from Féolan as she could. The sight of him filled her with such longing, she simply did not know how to be in the same room. Gone from the castle by dawn, she spent long hours in the hut where she dried and prepared herbal remedies or working in the Chênier clinic with Marcus. Nights she lay awake, fighting her heart.

Now she stood at the castle gate with her family, ready to bid their guests farewell. She squared her shoulders, grasping at the shreds of her composure and knew it would fail her.

Danaïs had kissed Solange, thanked Jerome gravely and bear-hugged her brother. Now he came to Gabrielle, soft brown eyes filled with gentleness.

"You will be in our hearts always."

Tears welled up and she could do nothing to stop them. Danaïs opened his cloak and enfolded her, pulling her close. An unlooked-for sense of strength and peace stole into her. A gift, from him to her. In her need, she did not wonder or question but simply accepted. In a while she stood and gave him a shaky smile.

"There, beautiful healer. One small thing can I do for thee." Danaïs touched his breast and turned to his horse.

Féolan. He stood before her, eyes dark with sorrow. I cannot hold you, Gabrielle thought, willing him to understand. I cannot hold you, or I will never let you go. Féolan put his hand to his heart and then held out his palm. Her hand reached out to meet his and in that gesture were all the words neither one could say. Féolan reached into his pouch, pulled out a folded parchment and tucked it into her hand. "If you ever need me," he whispered, and kissed her lightly on the brow.

Gabrielle stood watching the riders until they were out of sight. The tears flowed unheeded down her face as the urgent beat of her heart pleaded with her to follow, now, before it was too late. With a last brief appearance on the farthest rise in the road, the tiny figures vanished.

CHAPTER 9

HARVEST time came and went; the leaves changed color and began to fall—and the scouts did not return. Instead there came, on a brisk October day that promised night-frost, an envoy from La Maronne.

Jerome had bid his scouts stop first at Castle Drolet in Gaudette and deliver a message to the king, knowing that any invasion would surely advance through one of the passes in Maronnais territory. The reply the envoy bore was brief but encouraging:

Greetings Verdeau,

Having received your news of impending Greffaire attack, we thank you for this warning. Though skeptical of your source, we sent scouts to join your own in seeking confirmation. Their continued absence is ominous, if not conclusive. La Maronne musters for defense.

We seek a military alliance for the protection of the Krylian Basin and request a meeting to discuss these matters. Your town of Ratigouche would be convenient to both, also to Barilles and Gamier if they will come. Please confirm your agreement and name the date.

King Drolet II
La Maronne

Jerome's measured voice hung in the air of the study as he read aloud from the parchment. Dispensing with formality for this impromptu meeting, the king opened discussion with a single word.

"Well?"

"Drolet is not stupid," exclaimed Tristan. "He knows La Maronne will be hit first, and that if the Greffaires get through to our territory he will hardly be in a position to come to our aid. So his 'military alliance' amounts mainly to everyone helping him."

"That's true," said General Fortin. "But it doesn't matter. There will be no peace for Verdeau, or anyone else, if La Maronne is occupied by the Greffaires. Our own defense starts in the Maronnais passes."

"They will still pay more than anyone, Tristan," Gabrielle pointed out quietly. "They will pay in blood."

GABRIELLE HAD NOT allowed herself to play the lovelorn wretch. The ache in her heart was like a wound that crusts over but never really heals. Nights were the worst. A sudden memory as she hovered near sleep was enough to break the thin skin and start the wound bleeding again, and she awoke more than once with her pillow drenched in tears. But she could not float through life wan and tragic; she was a bonemender, and people needed her. Soon, they might need her even more. She threw herself into her work, dogging through long days that left her too tired to dream.

General Fortin had agreed that the bonemenders should be mobilized along with the military; and so, after all, Gabrielle had become involved in Verdeau's war plans. Before harvest-time she

had helped her father draft a decree directing all bonemenders
to prepare and store extra quantities of healing herbs, bandaging
and other supplies, and to provide a portion of these to their local
garrison. Each garrison had been asked to select a corps of men
to be trained in the basics of wound treatment—"so at least they
don't bleed to death being carried off the field," as Marcus grimly
put it—and Marcus had helped Gabrielle to reach bonemenders
throughout the country to provide this training.

Just before winter set in, Dominic came up from Blanchette,
while her father and General Fortin traveled to Ratigouche to
meet with the Maronnais. Gabrielle sat down with her brother to
decide how many bonemenders should travel with the defending
armies and where they should be deployed.

"It's sheer guesswork," she sighed, waving at their careful lists.
"Only your men, Dominic, have ever even been in a battle and
those were only pirate raids. None of us has any idea what to
expect."

"We know enough to expect it to be bad," said Dominic heavily.
"If there is war, Gabrielle, I fear we could empty the country of
bonemenders, and it would not be enough. Yet some must stay.
It's not only soldiers who suffer in wartime."

But not me, she vowed silently. She didn't know how she would
overcome her family's certain opposition, and she felt nothing but
dread at witnessing the carnage of a battlefield. Yet she knew in
her heart that she must go. Three times now the nightmare had
come, breaking through fatigue and heartache to jolt her awake
in horror. It was terrible, what she saw in the black of the night,
but she felt it as a summons. Gabrielle's gift, unique among the
bonemenders, would be needed. There was someone she was
going to have to save.

THE SNOW FELL, and autumn's feverish preparations cooled into a long uneasy wait.

"It doesn't seem real anymore," Gabrielle confessed to her mother a few days after Winter Solstice. "We sit here by the fire drinking tea, and I wonder sometimes if I imagined the whole thing. Or if this is a dream, this dark, brooding winter."

It was no dream, though, that Tristan had become a soldier. He trained, and stayed, with the Chênier garrison now and was home only for tactical meetings and relief days.

"He'll be an officer by spring," Fortin had reported to Jerome and Solange. "Not for his birth, but for his own merit. I feared he might be a little flighty, you know, but he is serious when he needs to be, and he's not afraid of hard work. He'll be the kind of leader men follow out of love, not fear."

With Tristan away and the bonemenders sorted as well as might be, Gabrielle found time heavy on her hands. She tried to keep busy with her patients and continued to help her mother manage the castle affairs, but the long quiet evenings crawled by. She was lonely. The pursuits that had always brought her comfort and contentment—music, wandering the hills with Cloud—now brought memories that made her lonelier still.

Relief came in the form of a messenger from Blanchette: Dominic's wife Justine was expecting another baby in about a month and insisted that Gabrielle midwife the birth. The whole family would be arriving in a few days and staying until snowmelt. Gabrielle was delighted.

Solange was glad too. She had observed the unfolding romance between Gabrielle and Féolan almost before they were aware of it themselves and had felt in her heart that this one, strange though he was to her, was right for her daughter.

She didn't know, still, quite what had gone wrong. The night the Elves had left she had held her daughter while she wept, but Gabrielle had said only that they were "too different." And perhaps they were. What did Solange know of Elves? She hadn't thought they still existed. She did know that Gabrielle was hiding a sadness that seemed to have sunk into her bones. A baby to birth and children to brighten up the house would do her good.

The two women set to work, ordering extra food, overseeing the preparation of two guest rooms, bringing Tristan's old cradle down from storage and having a new down ticking made for it. Solange went into town to buy special wool for baby clothes—it came from sheep raised in the Gamier foothills. The straight silky fleece was triple-washed and carded until it was soft as a cloud. New babies always set her to knitting like a fiend. Gabrielle wasn't much good with needlecrafts—at the age she should have been perfecting her skill, she had been apprenticing with Marcus instead. But she stocked in the practical things they would need for the birth and combed the shops for little toys and treats for the two older children. Her baby gift would wait until she had met the newborn babe.

Justine arrived in the late afternoon, tired from the journey but otherwise well. Her belly sailed in the door before her and was exclaimed over and patted in the flurry of greetings. Gabrielle marveled to think that on her last visit, back at FirstHarvest, the new baby had been a secret life still hidden from view. The children, four-year-old Matthieu and his sister, Madeleine, two years older, were restless from the long carriage ride and squirmed away from their grandmother's hugs, galloping off to explore the castle grounds.

"They'll be back," Justine said wryly, allowing herself to be installed on a long settee in the library. The family often gathered here instead of in the formal salon, for in addition to a wall filled with treaties and histories and the map case, the room boasted an oversized fireplace, games tables and vastly more comfortable (if less elegant) seating. "They didn't eat much at mid-day." Gabrielle pulled off Justine's boots and propped her swollen feet up on a deep down cushion at the end of the settee. "Mmm. Careful, Gabrielle, I'll fall asleep if I get too comfortable!"

At that Solange ordered "tea with luncheon" and sent Dominic out to round up his children. Leaving Justine with a cup of tea on the table beside her, they shooed the two youngsters into the small dining room where they ate their less formal meals. Madeleine slipped her hand into Gabrielle's as they walked.

"My mama says you're the best bonemender in all of the Basin," she chirped, swinging Gabrielle's hand.

Gabrielle laughed. "I'm sure that's not true, but it's nice of your mother to say so, don't you think?"

"No. It's not nice. She means it. And I said I think you're the prettiest of all the ladies, and I mean that too. I said I bet you could have lots of handsome husbands! Then Mama was cross and said people only have one husband. But Jeanne our cook had two husbands, so I think she must be wrong."

"Perhaps Jeanne's first husband died," suggested Gabrielle, steering away from the subject of her own marriage prospects.

"He did," confirmed Madeleine. "He fell off a ladder, and then he died. Jeanne cried for three weeks. I saw her crying in the kitchen. And then she married Leo. But you didn't marry anyone, did you?"

"No," said Gabrielle. "No, I didn't."

Solange rescued her. "Madeleine, sit up and eat now. Your mother said you didn't eat today, you two. How come?"

"The carriage made me throw up," said Matthieu cheerfully, loading up his plate.

DOMINIC'S ARRIVAL HAD triggered a new series of meetings. The coast was the best defended part of the country, and the question of whether to move all the coastal troops into the interior, leaving the Island and Blanchette virtually unguarded, was a vexing one.

Gabrielle overheard her brothers, still in heated conversation, as they emerged from one of these sessions. She was heading toward the clinic, her mind on the wet, fevered cough that was flaring up all over Chênier. Winter was a hard season, especially for the old ones.

A door clicked open, and Tristan's voice floated into the tiled hallway ahead of the two men. "I just don't think we should discount the Elves completely," Tristan was saying. "They live up there. They know the country. *Their* scouts didn't get captured. They should be our allies."

"Tristan, I doubt there are even enough of them to make a difference," replied Dominic. "And you said it yourself—they keep apart. We can't count on them. If we can't count on them for sure, then we shouldn't count on them at all."

"Féolan and Danaïs said they would try to persuade their Council to join in the defense," said Tristan stubbornly. "They believe the Elves should be part of this. I think we should at least invite them to a strategy meeting."

"I know they are your friends, Tris, but who knows if they have any influence over this Council? In any case, how would we contact them? Their settlements are secret, right? You could ride all over the Maronnais highlands and never find them."

Their voices faded away as they rounded a corner.

Gabrielle stood motionless for a minute. Then she turned, the clinic forgotten, and hurried upstairs to her chamber. She crossed the room to her bureau and took down the carved wooden box that sat there. It had been a gift from Dominic for her thirteenth birthday, and it still moved her that as a swaggering young man he had chosen something so right: a beautiful adult thing, with an elaborate key to appeal to a young girl's desire for secrets of her own. Tristan, only eight at the time, had given her a gaudy necklace, and she had been able to please both by declaring it would be the first treasure kept in her box.

Now she sat on the edge of her bed with the box on her lap, turned the key and lifted the lid. Tucked at the back was the scrap of parchment Féolan had left with her. Gabrielle took it out, unfolded it and smoothed it with her hands. How many times had she sat looking at the words he had written there? They gave directions—not right to the Stonewater settlement, "for that is forbidden without Council's permission," wrote Féolan—but to a sentry-point where a messenger could make contact. *If you ever need me.* Did Féolan mean for her to pass it on to the War Council? She thought not. But what if there was great need? Was not Verdeau's need her need also?

By then it will be too late for messengers, her mind replied.

CHAPTER 10

THE Elves of Stonewater had not been idle. They and the other Elvish settlements were not just well hidden; they had been well armed to start with, and over the winter the stores of weaponry grew steadily. Unlike the Humans, many Elves who had fought in the last war still lived, and their experience guided both training drills and strategy meetings.

It was all provisional, however; at this point the Elves intended to fight only if directly attacked, and they doubted the *Gref Orisé* would bother searching out their small territories.

Féolan was not able to counter these decisions, because he was not there. He was deep in *Gref Orisé* territory, attempting the most perilous scouting expedition of his life.

IT WAS A MISTAKE, OF COURSE. He knew it even as he was setting out, though he would not admit it to himself. A dark recklessness had come over him after leaving Gabrielle. Nothing much had seemed to matter, certainly not his own safety. But a deep anger had come over him on his last foray into the mountains when, instead of the enemy camp he had thought to observe, he had found only the remains of the five Human scouts who had arrived before him, their bodies hanging from the autumn trees like obscene fruit. The sight of those defiled bodies twisting in the wind had pushed him to it. He must do something against the tide of destruction poised above them.

The leaders of Stonewater Council had thought him mad.

"Féolan, it doesn't really matter if we don't know which pass they will come through. We prepare to defend our settlements only."

"But the Humans need to know. They have a long border; they can't possibly meet the *Gref Orisé* with enough men if they don't know where they will come over the mountains."

"Let the Humans scout out the information they need. It's ridiculous for you to take this risk."

"I might find out something important."

"More likely you will be captured and killed. You will be over there until snowmelt."

They had been right, but Féolan was deaf to their arguments. The truth was, he needed to go. The thought of spending the winter in Stonewater, cooped up with his own thoughts, was more than he could bear.

"Do you seek your own death?" Danaïs had demanded angrily when he heard of Féolan's intentions.

"Perhaps I seek a reason to live," Féolan replied softly, and Danaïs, who alone of his friends knew his sorrow over Gabrielle, sighed and touched his arm.

"May you find it then," he said, "and return to us safe."

Of course as a free citizen Féolan could travel where he would, and when Council saw he was determined, they had agreed to his one request, which was to have the clothing and equipment of the two *Gref Orisé* soldiers who had been taken prisoner the day he first discovered their camp. He spent weeks preparing, studying the *Gref Orisé* dialect from old accounts and the few Elves who had some knowledge of it. It was a form of Krylaise, but so far from Basin Krylaise as to be nearly another language. Féolan knew he would be many days in *Gref Orisé* before he could hope to speak without giving himself away as a stranger.

He left on a blustery, dark morning in tenthmonth, wearing the clothing but not the armor or insignia of one of the prisoners. The other outfit and a month's worth of travel biscuits were stored in a nondescript bag over his shoulder. He didn't dare carry anything as conspicuous as a sword, but a *Gref Orisé* knife was strapped to his belt, and he wore his own Elvish blade hidden against his skin. He had only his own cloak and blanket, which would have to be replaced in *Gref Oris* by something of local make. Danaïs rode with him into the foothills, leaving him at the mouth of the Skyway Pass.

"Will you not reconsider this fool's journey, Féolan?" asked his friend before they parted. "If you really want to help the Humans, why not lend your bow to their forces? I could stand beside you there."

Féolan replied with a grim smile. "This is ground we have trod before, Danaïs. Give it up now, and wish me all the luck and Elvish stealth I shall need."

"You know I do." The two men clasped hands, and Féolan slipped from his horse and began the winding climb through the mountains.

GABRIELLE PRESSED THE flared end of the little horn against Justine's belly, bent over, put the narrow end in her own ear and listened. Nothing. She moved the horn slightly, tried again. Yes. Faint but steady, faster than an adult's pulse—the baby's heartbeat. Eyes closed, finger keeping time so Justine could see, she listened to the rhythm for a full two minutes.

"Perfect. Banging away like a bell." She smiled at Justine. "Everything seems fine, Justine. I expect this birth will go as well as the others."

Justine smiled back, but Gabrielle could tell she was anxious. "Could I ask you to ... you know, do that thing you do, Gabrielle? Check things out, just to be sure? I have the oddest feeling about this baby."

"Of course. Let me see if I can sense anything." In this situation sense was a more comfortable word for most people than see, which is how Gabrielle thought of it herself. She cradled her hands around Justine's belly, closed her eyes and focused deep inside herself. Slowly her "vision" shifted, and she was inside Justine. She looked for infection or other problems and found nothing. Then she moved on to the baby. So strange how you could feel yourself moving within a separate being, a person within a person. Hello, baby, she thought, wondering if the baby could be aware of her presence. She let her inner sight rove over the unborn child, looking for trouble spots: the spine, the brain, the heart. The baby kicked and stretched under her hands, and the feeling she got from him (it was a boy, she knew, though she would keep the news to herself) was of robust health.

"Justine, the baby seems very well; you too. I can't promise I didn't miss anything, but I do have a strong feeling that you are both fine."

Justine searched her face. "You would tell me if you found anything?"

"I swear it. I'm as sure as I can be that the baby is healthy."

Justine relaxed visibly. "Thank-you, Gabrielle. Maybe I'm just nervous. This is the gloomiest winter, and who knows what is to come? Still, I feel a lot better knowing I'm having the baby here, with you."

ALMOST THREE WEEKS later, a voice woke her in the night.

"Gabrielle? I'm sorry to disturb you."

Gabrielle opened her eyes to find Justine, huge in her white nightgown, standing by her bed. She sat up, groped for a lamp and lit it.

"What is it, Justine? Is the baby coming?"

"I've only just started having pains. They aren't bad yet. But, Gabrielle, the baby's not right anymore. Look!"

"Let's get a bit more light first. Here, sit down." Gabrielle eased Justine down on her bed, then moved around the room lighting as many lamps as she could find. She brought them all over to her bedside table, then asked Justine to lie down. Even by flickering lamplight, she could tell at a glance that the baby had somehow got himself sideways. Justine looked like she had a watermelon wedged across her stomach. It was a comical sight, but Gabrielle knew this was no joke. A baby could be born bottom first, at need, but there was no way he could get out like that.

"Oh, you silly baby, what have you done," she murmured, trying to loosen the grip of Justine's fear. Justine was hovering on the edge of panic, but she gave a breathy little laugh.

"How on earth did he get like that? He seemed fine when I went to bed."

"I can't imagine." Gabrielle noticed that Justine was calling the baby "he." Her mother's intuition was right on two counts, then. "Maybe you're going to give birth to a contortionist rather than a prince or princess." She ran her hands slowly over the awkward lump, calming Justine and figuring out what part of the baby

was where. Her mind was racing. She would have to act fast. As
Justine's labor progressed—and it was likely to progress quickly
with a third baby—her womb would tighten up until the baby
was bound in that position, immovable. Even as she thought this,
she felt Justine's belly ripple and tighten under her hand. Just a
short contraction but a clear warning.

She would have to move the baby. She knew the risks: if the
birth cord was pinched, the baby could be harmed. If it was
pulled away from the wall of the womb, it could cause bleeding
that would endanger both Justine's and the baby's lives. But if
Gabrielle could shift him back into place safely—and she did
have an advantage over ordinary midwives on that count—then
once labor was well underway, he would stay put.

She explained the situation to Justine. Justine looked pale in
the dark room, her eyes wide and frightened. But she nodded at
Gabrielle's proposal. "That's why I came to you."

"Let's go get Dominic," suggested Gabrielle. "I'll have to pay
total attention to what I'm doing, and I want someone here to
keep you company."

As they walked together up the hall to Justine and Dominic's
chamber, Gabrielle prayed she would not end up doing more
harm than good.

CHAPTER 11

GREF ORIS was deep in winter's clutches before Féolan was ready to make his move. After six weeks spent lurking on the edges of Human settlements, sleeping rough in the bitter cold and eating little, Féolan was starting to look the half-starved peasant he was hoping to pass for. A chronic cough now roughened his voice, and the hair he had hacked short with his knife was a shaggy, unkempt mass that hung over his eyes and ears.

He had planned to live in the woods unnoticed, as he often had in the Basin, making only brief forays into villages and towns as he learned the ways and speech of the *Gref Orisé*. But once out of the foothills, the land on the other side of the mountains was mostly rolling, wind-swept plain, dusted now with snow and broken only with small patches of scrubby woodland. Even for an Elf, staying hidden in this land was near impossible. And he soon learned that here, no one would dare welcome or shelter a stranger.

It was an appalling country. Féolan had never before conceived of a place where oppression was the common condition of life, but in *Gref Oris* nearly everyone, it seemed, walked in fear. Only soldiers and the richest nobles traveled and spoke freely. Everyone else labored under the emperor's fist. The roads were full of checkpoints, manned by soldiers who demanded travelers' "papers" and explanations as to their business. All but the smallest villages were walled and gated, all who entered or left questioned. Always the questions were answered with bowed heads and cringing voices.

Because he could not risk the roads, Féolan's progress was slow. Still, he kept the roads in sight for he had no other means of finding any habitation. Each foray Féolan made to a market or town square started with a perilous midnight climb over the quietest stretch of the wall. It was long before he found a checkpoint with enough cover that he could sneak close and observe. There he had seen a young man pulled off the road, beaten and sent back the way he came, seemingly for setting off to see a girl without his master's permission. He had seen an entire family arrested and dragged off in chains, for what crime, he could not say.

That day, he had almost decided to turn around and take his chances crossing back over the winter mountains. He could do nothing here. His original plan—to volunteer for the army as a means of learning something of the *Gref Orisé* battle plan—was impossible without identity papers. He knew now the army was mustering at a camp just north of the foothills, had overheard both individual men and uniformed units give it as their destination to the sentries. But he would learn nothing more, unless he could be a ranked soldier in a regular regiment. He could waylay some civilian traveler and rob him of his papers, but he had no stomach for treachery. He would just try to get home and report to his Council that invasion was, indeed, on its way.

Fate intervened in the form of a corpse. Féolan was heading back to the little hollow in a strip of trees where he was camped, a task that demanded three hours of crawling, sometimes on hands and knees, sometimes right down on his belly, across stubbly grainfields and pastureland. He was within sprinting distance of the little wood when he noticed the crows circling and squabbling a few hundred yards away. He watched, motionless in the snow. When a couple of vultures sailed in to investigate, he was certain: something dead was lying at the edge of the field.

Even then, he wasn't expecting a man. He was thinking rather that if it was a decent-sized animal and seemed reasonably fresh, he might risk making a fire and eating it. The few *Gref Orisé* coins he had found in the pockets of his "borrowed" clothes had not been enough to buy more than a threadbare woolen coat and a meager supply of the cheapest food, certainly not meat. He was always hungry now.

The man was heavily built, well but not richly dressed. He lay pitched face-first in the snow, frostbite obvious on the exposed skin. The crows had begun their work, Féolan noticed with distaste, but there were no signs that the man had died violently. Hoofprints all around made it clear that he had arrived on a small horse or mule, though it had left without him. Rich enough to ride, then.

Féolan scanned his surroundings as he considered this windfall. It was risky. If the man was important enough to be known, an imposter would be recognized and caught. But if he was, as Féolan hoped, a middle-ranking, unremarkable person—say a successful farmer or tradesman—that could be the identity he needed. Quickly, he checked the man's pockets. The coat yielded only a pair of stiff leather gloves. Féolan dragged the man over onto his back and opened the coat. There was a pocket in the front of the man's tunic, and a small pouch strung on a rope around his middle. The pouch contained a generous handful of coins. The pocket contained a square of heavy parchment—identity papers.

Féolan did not risk checking the papers there. He lifted the corpse under its arms and hauled it into the woods. He returned with an evergreen branch and, following the hoofprints out about a hundred boot-lengths, swept the snowy tracks away as well as he could. A good wind would finish the job.

That night, Féolan traveled by darkness as far from the dead man as he could get. He was headed south, back toward the mountains, not to escape, but to join the muster. He wasn't sure yet exactly where it was, but once he got close, the flow of traffic would lead him there. He wore the clothes and papers of a black-smith named Brakar. Like many of his people, Féolan had some knowledge of metalwork. He knew how to make arrowheads, knife blades and jewelry. He hoped it would be enough.

THE BABY DIDN'T want to turn. Gabrielle had mapped out his position and followed the line of the birth cord in her mind. To her relief, everything looked all right for a safe reposition-ing. Deeply focused on the baby, she waited until Justine's belly relaxed after a contraction, and then slowly but firmly pressed down on the baby's head with one hand and up at the bottom end with the other. She kept up the pressure until Justine gasped, but the baby didn't budge. Were the walls of the womb already too tight?

Gabrielle reached up and squeezed Justine's shoulder. She had made her sister-in-law as comfortable as she could on the big feather bed, tucking pillows under her knees and arms and encouraging Dominic to climb right up beside her. Still, she could feel Justine's tension.

"I'm sorry, Justine; it didn't work that time." Justine's eyes welled up.

Dominic's mouth tightened with fear.

"Don't lose heart," Gabrielle urged. "This is only our first try. I just wonder if... Justine, do you think you could get up on your knees? On the floor maybe, leaning over the side of the bed. I want to get the baby away from your backbone, make as much room as possible. See if we can use the pull of the earth to help us."

"Where will you be?" asked Justine.

"Ah... I'm not sure. Let's see if we can figure it out."

Minutes later, Justine was draped over the bed, and Gabrielle was wedged beneath her on the carpeted floor, her head in the dust balls. If this works, she thought, we'll have something to laugh over later. Leaving her fear and her awkward position behind, she closed her eyes, placed her hands on Justine's belly and let the world fade away. This time she tried to make contact with the baby. The words were in her head, but what she hoped to send were feelings and pictures: comfort, love and the image of a head-down baby all ready to be born. Hello, sweetheart. It's me again. You're going to meet your momma soon. You know your momma. She loves you. But first you have to wiggle down. Feel how heavy your head is, it's soooo heavy it's going to sink way down so your feet can float up. Are you ready? Now dooown goes that head! She pushed. The head slid downward, slowly, so slowly. Gabrielle did not hurry, just kept the pressure steady and sent the baby warmth and love. Vaguely, far away, she heard Justine making little excited sounds as she realized the baby was moving. Listen, baby. You're making your momma happy. Everything will be fine now.

Sylvain DesChênes was born at sunrise and was as healthy as Gabrielle had predicted. He was pronounced "cute" by his older sister, "squishy-looking" by his older brother and "perfect" by his grandmother. His mother didn't call him anything. She just held him close, barely letting go long enough to break her fast. Dominic, who had never flown his feelings in the breeze like Tristan, surprised Gabrielle by wrapping her in a fierce hug in the privacy of the hallway. "Thank-you. Thank-you. Gods above, Gabrielle, I can't bear to think what would have happened without you."

CHAPTER 12

"YOU'RE scrawny for a smith."

That was an understatement. Though taller than most Humans and broad-shouldered, Féolan had been slight for a smith to start with. After weeks of short rations, he was scrawny, period. But he had expected the comment, and now, having been directed by a checkpoint guard to a huge garrison sprawled just a half-day's march from the mouth of the Skyway Pass, he prepared to brazen it out.

Féolan nodded and gave the sneering officer what he hoped was an embarrassed grin. "Th-th-that's what my f-f-father do say," he blurted out. He had affected a stutter to give him an excuse for speaking little. Already he was mightily tired of it, but it did seem to distract people from his accent. "H-h-he thought I'd n-n-n-e'er make a, a sm-m-mith."

Open laughter from the men nearby greeted this pronouncement. Féolan ducked his head, as though shamed. What kind of people laugh at a stranger's affliction? he thought.

The recruiting officer was unimpressed. "Think you can fight then, do you?" he demanded.

"Aye, sir. I-I-I'm strong, and f-f-f-fast." Féolan hoped this was still true. He'd eaten well the past two days, thanks to Brakar's coins, but he was hardly in fighting form.

"Here then!" A battle-ax flew toward him. Startled, he threw his arm up and caught it. Instantly the officer was upon him, swinging his own ax down toward Féolan's head. Féolan parried, awkward but fast as promised. A good thing. The force of the blow was vicious. It seemed that in *Gref Oris* the way to fail as a prospective army recruit was to be killed.

They fought a few minutes longer, Féolan parrying and blocking but careful not to attack his would-be superior officer. The battle-ax was a lucky choice, he decided. It was an unfamiliar weapon for him, so he seemed what he claimed to be, an able but untrained fighter.

"You'll do." The officer shoved his ax in a barrel behind him and motioned Féolan to do the same. "Go with Garran, here. He'll get you outfitted and barracked. Dismissed."

Féolan wondered if he should give some sign of fealty, but the officer had already turned his back, and Garran was striding off across the crowded yard.

DAYS PASSED BEFORE Féolan felt secure enough to sleep soundly. He had to be on his guard at all times: to hide his skill with a sword; to stay in one piece during battle-ax sparring; to avoid lapsing into Elvish gestures or Basin Krylaise; to copy the *Gref Orisé* manner of eating, polishing weaponry and addressing superiors. At night, he remained on guard against those who had no qualms about robbing the new man while he slept. These attempts soon died down, however, as word got out that the skinny new recruit slept but lightly and was devilish quick with his knife.

The stutter turned out to be more hindrance than help. The soldiers of *Gref Oris* were a taciturn bunch; no excuse was required for keeping silent or to oneself. It was a grim, cheerless place, and as he lay on his pile of dirty straw at night, listening to the rustles and snores around him, he longed as never before for his own home and friends. In the quietest hours, the image of Gabrielle would come to his mind, and somehow her memory brought comfort along with the sorrow.

When not training, he was sometimes put to repairing weaponry and armor, and he had feared at first that this would be his downfall, for he knew nothing of making armor. Neither, it turned out, did any other civilian blacksmith. Armory was the military's domain, as were swords and axes, and the Chief Smith would not let him touch a piece of equipment until he had been shown exactly what was expected. He was in far greater danger with the tack for the horses and had almost given himself away the first time he had been asked to replace a stirrup.

Féolan observed carefully and worked with diligence. Though the labor was brutally hot and heavy, it was the one place where he had a chance of overhearing important news. The enlisted men he trained and bunked with were either too stolid or too frightened to ask questions; in any case, he heard none of the speculation and rumors that he had expected about the upcoming invasion. Even when the men gambled in the evening, pulling out their tin flasks of corn liquor, their tongues rarely loosened. The smithy, though, was a kind of crossroads, where men in charge of weapons, armor, horses and supplies met and where officers were custom-fitted. That made, on occasion, for some interesting talk—already he had heard a horse-master speculate that "we'll be lucky to get even a few over that pass"—so Féolan set himself to become the Chief Smith's first choice when help was required.

And so he did. The man, himself massive in the arms and shoulders, had been unimpressed with Féolan's weight, but the precision of his work was another matter. Féolan took easily to the fussy business of molding the armor pieces to the curve of a man's body and could quickly and neatly replace the fine link chain and buckled leather strapping that held the various plates together.

He was soon noticed in the training field, as well. It was risky to show his skill too early, but Féolan had soon realized that he had little hope of discovering anything at the lowest rank, so he allowed his swordsmanship to "progress" beyond his fellow recruits. Yet every advance increased the danger of lapsing into a move that was Elvish, rather than *Gref Orisé*, and betraying himself.

So Féolan's heart thudded with alarm when, three weeks after his arrival and after neatly besting his partner in the ring, a loud voice thundered, "You! Brakar." Turning slowly, head in the required bow, Féolan thought desperately of escape.

"Sir?"

A burly officer faced him.

"Follow me."

They marched through the camp, Féolan wondering at every step if he hurried to his own death. Ten minutes later, they entered the armory.

"Another to be outfitted," his brusque guide announced and strode out the door.

"Step forward, soldier." This from the impatient armory clerk. Féolan stepped forward. The clerk recognized Féolan from the smithy and brightened slightly. "Been awarded a suit, eh? Good on you!"

Well, it was an opening and openings were, as they said here, rare as good fortune. He took his chances.

"D-d-don't everyw-w-one gets one?"

The clerk snorted. "Not hardly. Ain't got suits for the whole world, have we? Bloody expensive, they are. Suits goes to the good fighters, the ones to keep alive. The other enlisted men get helmets and whatever bits an' pieces are left over. The conscripts—oh, not many here yet, but there be throngs afore long—they get nothin'."

Blessed starshine, the man's a talker, Féolan thought. "N-n-n-o weapons, ev-v-ven?" he ventured.

"Spread out so I can measure ya. Oh, they'll get weapons of a sort, when they head into the field. Not before."

"W-w-w-on't be good f-f-fight-fighters, then," observed Féolan, obediently stretching out his arms and legs.

"Nor do they have to be." The clerk flashed him a wolfish grin. "Be glad you signed up. Your job's to fight. The conscripts' job is just to get in the enemy's way. After the enemy kills a couple thousand, he's plumb wore out, isn't he? Might turned to shite." He sniggered at his own joke. "Then our armored warriors come at them."

Féolan nodded thoughtfully. Ten minutes later, he was headed to the smithy to be fitted for his suit.

CHAPTER 13

S YLVAIN stretched, grimaced, puckered his mouth as though to cry, seemed to think better of it and opened his eyes instead. He was in Gabrielle's arms, and he stared up at her with a searching gaze that pulled at her heart. She could not return a newborn's intent stare or feel the weight and heat of his head in her hand without imagining how it would be to hold one of her own. Such longing was the bittersweet cost of midwifing babies, and she accepted it as fair price.

She smiled at Sylvain now, joggling him gently in her arms. Justine, sleeping upstairs, would soon be needed for feeding duty, but now the baby was content. Solange, still knitting in the chair beside Gabrielle, looked at him hungrily. Gabrielle laughed. "If I wanted to torture you, all I would have to do is keep holding this baby!" She walked over and gave the baby up into his grandmother's eager arms. Solange tucked the downy head under her chin and rocked, eyes closed.

"Justine seems to be doing well," she said, her words a question.

"Yes, fine," answered Gabrielle. "She's tired, of course, but that's to be expected. It was a good birth." It had been too, once the baby was straightened around. Gabrielle had felt contented and peaceful ever since. A healthy birth never failed to fill her with wonder.

"Momma..."

"Hmmm?" Solange was taken up with her rocking, not paying much attention. Maybe this wasn't the right time. "What is it, Gabrielle?"

"It's just... well, you've never told me about my own birth. I just wondered how it went for you. Was it difficult? Did you have a good helper? You know, things like that."

There was a long silence. Gabrielle hadn't meant to upset her mother but for some reason she had.

"Mother, I'm sorry if... it doesn't matter. We don't have to..."

"No, Gabrielle, it's all right," Solange replied. "It's time I told you. Past time, maybe." She seemed frightened, Gabrielle realized with confusion. Solange rose from her chair and tiptoed the baby over to the little cradle on the floor. "Luckily this one has decided to sleep some more. Close the door, dear, so we won't be interrupted."

Mystified, Gabrielle did as she was bid.

"I hardly know how to begin this," said Solange. "I have worried so long about whether and how to tell you. When I heard war was coming, I felt I must, but I've been avoiding it, I suppose."

What under the stars was she talking about? Gabrielle knew no ordinary birth story could cause Solange such anxiety. What, then? She fought back the urge to interrupt.

"The year you were born, your father and I moved the court to Blanchette for more than a year. There had been a lot of pirate raids along the coast, and Jerome hadn't full faith in the Regent at the time; you know Jerome, he thinks no one can handle things as well as he can. So, we moved so he could improve the coastal defenses and reassure the people.

"I became pregnant while we were there. I was more than half-way along when we were due to return to Castle DesChênes. But a couple of days before our departure... well, I lost the baby."

Gabrielle knew her mother was prone to miscarry: she had been old enough to understand the two miscarriages that had occurred after Tristan's birth. How painful those losses must have been for her! Something in Solange's face stopped Gabrielle from sharing her sympathy, though. Her mother was not interested in pity; she was inside the story.

"It was the first time, and I was devastated. I couldn't face all those people knowing—the court, the servants, the Blanchette nobles. I just wanted to hide. So I insisted to Jerome that we say nothing, just leave as planned. He wanted me to stay on and rest, but I wouldn't. We said I had suffered a slight illness, and a day later we left.

"But I was so sad. And our big convoy back to Chênier—there was no comfort there. Jerome was wonderful. He asked if I wouldn't like to spend a few days with him at his grandfather's summerhouse, just us. Time to heal before heading back to the bustle of the castle. Of course I said yes!"

The scene was vivid in Gabrielle's mind: Solange a young, dark-eyed queen, struggling with a private sorrow and a public position. The relief with which she would welcome a brief retreat from the world. But how Gabrielle herself fit into this story was a mystery still. She did not ask. She held herself still, and listened.

"So we sent everyone on to Chênier, even little Dominic and his nurse, and kept only a couple of bodyguards and a maidservant with us. Oh, Jerome's master-at-arms was not happy about it! But he argued in vain, and we set off alone.

"The house was just down the coast, toward the Pickerel River, less than a morning's easy ride. Soon after we left, the road veered away from the ocean and ran through a forested area. I remember thinking how lovely the shade felt, how quiet it was. So soothing. And then we came upon the most terrible scene. I couldn't believe what I was seeing at first—dead people, Gabrielle, five or six of them, murdered and left lying where they fell. It was ... I can't tell you how awful.

"I turned away off the path, sickened, while the men debated what to do. And that's when I heard, just faintly, a baby's cry. I thought, That's it, I've gone completely crazy. But my maid heard it too, and we followed the sound to a huge hollow log lying just off the road."

Solange looked up from her hands, directly at Gabrielle. "It was you, Gabrielle. You were tucked into the log. I remember feeling I was in a dream as I reached in to take you out. You were so tiny. I had never felt anything so soft as the shawl you were wrapped in. And then I was holding you, and your eyes stared up at me and they were like pools of deep water dancing with light, and I think I just fell in love with you right then and there."

Gabrielle stared. She reached for something, anything, to say. "But what had happened?"

"We never found out for sure. The people had been ambushed by marauders, most likely. The pirates had become very bold that year and did sometimes venture inland. I imagined your mother just having time to hide you away, praying that you would be overlooked ...

"Anyway, we took you to the house. The maid and I stayed while the men went back to see the bodies decently buried. And they—and this is the oddest part—they asked in all the nearby villages and farms, but nobody knew who the people were. Nobody was missing or expected. They were complete strangers.

"I don't know exactly when I became determined to have you for my own. Maybe that first time I looked at you, or maybe it grew in me day by day. I didn't want you raised as an orphaned kitchen girl. I wanted you to be mine. And somehow, I persuaded your father. We returned to Chênier a few weeks later with a baby. After eighteen months away, nobody thought it strange. Dominic had known a baby was coming, so your appearance made perfect sense to him. And we didn't visit the coast again for two years.

"To this day I don't know how it worked out. The first time someone asked me your birthday, and I made it up, my heart pounded so hard that I thought I would faint. But no one ever questioned my word. Hardly anyone knew, you see, how we had found you."

"Who was the maid?" asked Gabrielle. But she knew.

"Your nurse, Ella," confirmed Solange. And then her lip trembled, and she was crying. "Oh, Gabrielle, if I did wrong not to tell you, I'm sorry. When you were little, there seemed no way to explain so you would understand. And then, when you were older, it seemed too late. And, if I am honest, I was afraid to tell you. I just wanted to be your real mother."

"You are my real mother!" Gabrielle spoke hotly as if defending her mother against unknown accusers. "You saved my life. You loved me. You raised me as a daughter of House DesChênes. I don't care if I was born on the moon, *you* are my mother!"

It was the only thing she was sure of. The rest was in turmoil. Solange was weeping now with relief, and as Gabrielle went over to hold her, she didn't know if her mother's story changed everything, or nothing. She would have to go over it in her heart many times before she understood.

CHAPTER 14

FÉOLAN sat outside his barracks, polishing his armor.
He loathed it. It made him feel trapped, not protected,
and the thought of doing battle in such a lumbering getup
filled him with panic. Every strength and skill he relied on when
fighting—speed, agility, precision, his keen eyesight and hear-
ing—was hampered by the awkward weight of the metal casing.

Well. He wouldn't be enduring it much longer.

Féolan reviewed in his mind all he had learned. He was relieved
that the information he had gathered from the Stonewater Elves
who had fought the *Gref Orisé* in the last war and passed on to the
Verdeau Council was accurate. As far as he could tell, there were
still no archers among the *Gref Orisé*. Their armor seemed little
changed from the descriptions he had heard, and from his work
at the smithy he guessed that, as before, it could be pierced by
arrows but only from a heavy bow at close range. And the armor
plates were still, for the most part, attached by leather, which
could, potentially, be broken with a skilled or lucky thrust.

He knew more now. He knew there would be relatively few
horsemen due to the difficulties of traversing the mountain
passes. Nor would the *Gref Orisé* travel in armor, unless they
anticipated attack. (And now he knew why!) When they came

over the mountains, the conscripts would be carrying the heavy armor, saving the regular soldiers' strength for fighting.

The business of the conscripts was new too, and Féolan wondered what use could be made of this information. The defending army, ideally, should concentrate its efforts on the trained soldiers who came in the second wave. But how could the front ranks safely be ignored or avoided? He felt pity for these men, who had been pouring into the camp over the last week and were kept in a guarded compound. Their fate was to be a Human shield, killed brutally for a cause that availed them nothing.

And he had learned, finally, what he had come here to discover. He'd been working at the forge when Commander Col himself strode past. One of his officers was having a breastplate made, and seeing him there Col stopped. "Oh, Ryvent. Be at my tent at four bells, strategy meeting. The last troops are arriving next week."

"The other passes will still keep sentry forces as we discussed, though, Sir?" asked the unfortunate Ryvent.

He was rewarded with a fierce glare. "We discuss these matters in my tent because they are not for general broadcast, Ryvent. Control your mouth."

Féolan had already guessed by the sheer size of the garrison that there would be a single, focused thrust through the mountains. Now he was certain.

It was time to go. He hadn't learned anything of great import, but if he could get across the mountains in time he could, perhaps, tell the Humans where to gather their armies. And he had something to tell his own people too. If the *Gref Orisé* conquered the Basin, Elvish life would be forever changed. They might hide in the forest for a long time, but they would never again roam free and unhindered.

GABRIELLE LOOKED OUT over the battlements, shivering in her cloak. It was a still clear night, piercingly cold. Moonlight flooded silver over the snow. Another full moon. It was nearly two months since Sylvain's birth. Despite the cold, winter's grip on Verdeau was weakening. The days were longer and milder now, and on sunny days the icicles dripped, and the roads became treacherous with slush and mud. Soon snowmelt would begin in earnest, and the Verdeau armies would be on the move.

She thought back to that afternoon's War Council. The troops, she had been told, would start to muster in a fortnight and begin the trek to the Krylian foothills by month's end. They would take up their position before the mountains were passable.

"But where?" she had asked.

"That's the question which has occupied us through this long winter," said General Fortin. "We do not know where the Greffaires will cross over: at one of the three passes, or perhaps all. We must be prepared at each pass, yet dividing our forces increases the chance that they will break through and advance into Verdeau.

"The western pass, on our side at least, is narrow and treacherous. It would be most difficult to move a sizeable army through it. The Maronnais are posting a small sentry force there, with a standing request to Barilles to send reinforcements. The middle and eastern passes both seem possible. We will guard the Skyway Pass, the Maronnais the Eastern Gateway—again with a request to Gamier for additional troops. We also need to leave a sizeable force within Verdeau, in case we fail to stop them in the foothills."

"What if they don't come, after all this?" It was Poutin. "What if all this fuss and expense is for nothing?"

"Then we will have erred on the side of caution, and we will hope the people will forgive us," said Jerome impatiently. "They will not forgive us, on the other hand, if we allow them to be slaughtered through carelessness."

"They will come." Gabrielle surprised herself by voicing what she had only meant to think.

"What makes you so sure?" snapped Poutin.

How she wished she had said nothing. "I have dreamed it," she confessed, bracing herself for Poutin's scorn. But the memory of the dream that had stalked her sleep through the long winter must have been reflected in her face because Poutin on the verge of ridicule, fell silent.

In her dream, Gabrielle struggled to join together a rising tide of dismembered bodies. They were everywhere, awash with blood—legs, arms, trunks and the worst, the heads, crying out and imploring her—and the more she tried to match them up and piece them together, the more they piled up around her. In the backdrop of her dream, the battle raged, unseen but terrifying, unquestionably real. She was sure now. The Greffaires were coming.

"Dominic stays with the reserve army, at the crossroads north of Chênier," continued Jerome. "He is charged with the defense of Verdeau proper and the royal seat. Tristan and I will travel to La Maronne to meet the enemy. Gabrielle, it is time to call in the bonemenders who will serve our forces and decide who stays with the home force and who travels to the central pass."

Gabrielle had nodded agreement. She had not revealed her intention to undertake the journey herself.

She would go, though. The only question was how.

NOW GABRIELLE LEANED over the north wall of the tower
and found the silvery gleam of the Avine River. Pulling her cloak
tight around her shoulders, she stared at the northern horizon, just
a guessed-at shape of denser black against the night sky. Would
Elf eyes see the contours of the land clearly, she wondered, even
in the dark? Danaïs and Féolan had once pointed out a goshawk
that was no more than a black speck in the sky. Gabrielle had
thought they were pretending, teasing her, until they had proved
their skill. Standing against the far wall of her clinic, each had
read aloud from a heavy, leather-bound herbal that she held open
against her chest. At that distance, all she could see was a mean-
ingless blur on the page.

Gabrielle imagined the journey upriver, through the farthest
reaches of La Maronne to the edge of the Krylians. She thought
of the Greffaires, preparing for war, unseen behind the curtain of
the mountains. And she thought of Féolan and his people, hidden away in the forests and valleys of the Maronnais highlands.
Did they too prepare for war?

IN THE WARMTH of her chamber, Gabrielle lit a fire in the tiny
stove, wrapped a blanket over her nightgown and sat herself on the
thick patterned rug before the fire. There was no point in trying
to sleep yet, not with her mind so full of questions.

A sudden wail from Sylvain drifted down the hall, followed by
the muffled voices of his parents. Having Dominic's family here
had saved her, she thought. Justine and her baby, the two children,
had provided the best possible distraction from her own disquiet.
Madeleine and Matthieu blew through the castle like a couple
of charming whirlwinds, full of life and laughter and endless
demands. And Justine had always been a good friend.

But oh, she missed Tristan. He alone of her family, unimpressed by her grave demeanor and strange power, brought out her playfulness and sense of humor. She missed his teasing as much as she missed his warm heart. He had stayed to dinner tonight, shoveling in an astonishing amount of food. "Don't they feed you at the barracks?" she had demanded.

"They feed us lots, but they don't feed us well. Not like this," he had explained. "I need to dig deep while I can."

"Careful you don't throw up like I did," cautioned Matthieu.

"Never you fear, my lad. I can hold my grub with the best of them," boasted Tristan, grinning through a mouthful of pheasant. He reached past his older brother and tickled Matthieu in the ribs, then had to tickle Madeleine under the table just to be fair. The two children squirmed and giggled. It would be a long time, perhaps, before they would share such a light-hearted family meal again.

And she missed Féolan, still. His memory was sharp as a shard of glass. Gabrielle went to the carved box and pulled out the tiny necklace her mother had given her. "You were wearing it when I found you," Solange had explained. "I tried to save the shawl too, but the mice got into the trunk where it was stored."

The necklace was silver, the finest work she had ever seen. Tiny oval links led to a polished green stone, small as a droplet, embedded in a delicate silver setting. Gabrielle held it now in the palm of her hand. It made her feel strange to feel it on her skin, to think it had once circled her own neck. Sometimes when she held it she imagined things—snatches of song, voices, a woman's eyes—and would then put it away hurriedly, ashamed of the weakness that made her draw memories out of her own wishful thinking.

CHAPTER 15

THE garrison was more heavily guarded now that the invasion was imminent, for conscripts were not the only ones who might lose their nerve and desert. Féolan, reasoning the best way to slip past a sentry was to *be* the sentry, had volunteered for duty but been denied because of his stutter. A bitter jest, he thought, that a charade meant to protect him should cost so dear.

He was not especially worried about getting out. He could move as silently as a cat, and his own cloak, which despite the risk he had kept buried at the bottom of his kit against this day, would be almost invisible on a dark night. He was worried about speed. If they came after him on horseback, he would soon be overtaken and might be trapped in the pass with no cover. Trying to find another route through the mountains in late winter would be slow at best and might well be fatal. Yet he must stay ahead of the invasion force.

Could he take a horse? The chances of leaving secretly with a horse were slim, and once the foothills became treacherous, a horse would slow him down at night. His own night vision would serve him better. Féolan decided he would have to go on foot.

The moon had waned to a quarter. He could not wait for it to be gone altogether. On a day when the sky was layered with thick gray cloud promising a night rain that would, with any luck, both limit the sentries' vision and distract them with their own discomfort, he made his decision. He would leave that night.

HE WAS CAREFUL in the ring that day, not wanting to draw any last-minute attention to himself. Yet not even the most wary can guard against freak accidents.

It happened during a one-on-one sparring match. He had just delivered a powerful swing with the battle-ax, the kind of heavy blow his training commander approved of. It took a lot of power to slice through armor, though to his mind it was a lumbering stroke, easy to anticipate and avoid. He slowed it down just the same, enough to ensure his partner had time to duck or parry.

The two axes clashed together with a force that jolted Féolan's shoulder. And then the jarring collision was suddenly released as his ax-head flew free of its shaft and sailed through the air.

"'Ware!" shouted the trainer, but the warning came too late. A soldier, released from the field, helmet under his arm, was stowing his weapons in the arms barrels. The heavy ax-head clipped the top of his head, stuck there for one grisly second and then thudded to the ground. Féolan had a queasy glimpse of a red flap of scalp before the soldier crumpled, hands clapped around his head.

Féolan leaped to his side. "On my honor, man, I am sorry!" He ripped off his own helmet and gauntlets, laid a steadying hand on the man's back. "Can I help you to the surgeon's?" He looked to the training commander, expecting a nod of permission, and his own scalp prickled at the man's narrowed, suspicious glare.

Mistake on mistake. You let your guard down, he accused himself. Never mind the disappearance of the stutter, "On my honor" was a phrase he had never heard here. He didn't even know if the Basin Humans used it.

"DAMN YOUR EYES!" A heavy gauntlet collided against Féolan's temple, clutched at him, ripped. Féolan felt a flare of pain, and the injured man fell back into his own blood with a fistful of dark hair dangling from his glove. Along with the hair, Féolan saw with alarm, was the braided string he tied around his head to keep his chopped hair out of his eyes and over his ears. His hand flew to the spot. There was little hair left there to smooth down.

"You better hope I don't recover," the wounded soldier snarled. "Cuz when I do, I'll bloody kill you for this. Stuttering half-wit!"

Féolan stood, hoping the outburst had been enough to distract the trainer, and jammed the helmet back on his head. Perhaps, he told himself, they would return to their exercises.

"Brakar." Or perhaps not. Féolan turned, cursing his carelessness. Three guards, swords drawn, now flanked his commanding officer. "Remove your armor."

Wordlessly, Féolan stripped down. Free of armor, he could outrun all of these men, but he saw no hope of fighting his way through the entire camp. The training commander swaggered up to him.

"Where are you from, soldier?"

"P-p-p-agstak, Suh, Suh, Sir." Lay it on thick, lad. The thought was a bitter sneer. That stutter just cooked your goose, but maybe it will hide the fact that you don't know how to pronounce your hometown.

"Pah-pah-pah," the trainer imitated. "Lot of freaks in Pagstak, are there?" The contempt in the man's face gave Féolan sudden hope. It didn't strike him as a look one would give a dangerous spy. "Maybe people with webbing between their toes and one leg longer than the other? More people with animal ears? Or is it just you?" Sniggers rippled among the men, and Féolan ducked his head in apparent shame.

"Take him to the brig," the trainer told the guards. "The man smells off as old meat. How'd a defective blacksmith from Pagstak learn to fight like he does, anyway? He's hiding something, I'd bet my last bottle on it. I don't want him back here until he's been questioned and cleared."

"ABSOLUTELY NOT."

Jerome's face was red with anger. He had just been presented with Gabrielle's list of recruited bonemenders.

"Father, it makes sense." Appealing to Jerome's reason didn't seem a promising approach, but Gabrielle felt bound to try. "The bonemenders who go to the mountains must be fit and able-bodied themselves to make the journey and then work long and hard without a break. From within that group, we chose first those who were unwed, without children." She gave her father a level glance. "That's me." Jerome was about to cut in, but she hurried on.

"Plus, they need a leader. These bonemenders are used to working alone. Here they will need to work in a team. Someone has to organize the clinic area, figure out who does what and what goes where."

"Oh, and I suppose you are the only person who can do this?"

"Not the only person," said Gabrielle. "But I have organized the process thus far. I believe they would accept me as their leader."

"No. You will not go."

"Father." She was down to her last card. "Father, I am not some little boy, imagining war is a great adventure. I truly have no wish to see any of it. But I believe that I must go. I can't explain it well, but I feel certain I will be needed."

"I care not for your dreams and peculiar feelings!" Jerome was storming now, striding about the room. "It is enough that I put my son's life on the line. I will not have my daughter wallowing in the muck of war as well!" He left the study abruptly, leaving Gabrielle talking to herself.

"What if it were your son who needed me?"

CHAPTER 16

FÉOLAN cast an eye over his cellmates. Huddled on a filthy dirt floor, most without so much as a cloak for warmth, they nevertheless all appeared to be asleep.

Féolan would not be sleeping this night. His one stroke of luck had been the gaoler's decision to send him for questioning the following day. "You'll be a better talker after a couple of missed meals and a night with us, I'll warrant," he had said. Féolan did not intend to find out if the man was right. Come daybreak, he would be long gone—or dead.

The brig was not much to boast of—an ill-constructed cabin, minded at night by a single bored guard. It was not a true prison. It was used rather to punish laziness, insubordination and incompetence, so there was little need for elaborate precautions against escape. The lock was crude, embedded right into the door.

Slumped against the back wall, Féolan waited for his moment. He let his fingers play over the graceful curve of the Elvish knife hasp, still smooth against his shin. Two strokes of luck, after all. They apparently thought so little of him that they had done only a cursory pat down for hidden weapons.

His senses crackled to the alert as the guard stretched and yawned at his little table, pushed his chair back with a grunt and padded to the bucket that served as a urinal at the far end of the guardroom. Féolan had flitted silently to the door before the man had unbuttoned himself. The slim blade tip slipped into the keyhole, and deft Elvish fingers and sensitive ears found the catch in seconds. Féolan winced at the loud click as the lock released, but it must have been no louder in the guard's ears than the splash of his water in the tin bucket, for he never looked up.

The cell door would creak. He would have to make his exit in one swift spring. Now! Féolan sprinted—through the door and past the table in a bound—and had planted his knife in the guard's throat before his confused cry could rouse the alarm. Stopping only to grab the guard's cloak off the chair and throw it over his own shoulders, he eased out the main door of the brig.

Pressed against the back wall of the building, Féolan took stock. No one moved in this part of the camp, though he knew the sentries would be pacing out the perimeter. Silent as a shadow, he worked his way from one pool of blackness to the next.

He would have to get rid of a sentry as well as the guard. He needed time to cross a large plain unnoticed, and for that he needed a hole in their sight lines. He had already picked out a spot at the northeast corner of the garrison on the far side from the road to the pass; it offered better cover than the closer sentry points and would give the impression he was running back into *Gref Oris*. He planned to circle widely around the garrison and pick up the road to the pass in the foothills.

It was quickly done. Féolan waited in the lea of a building until the sentry came by on his rounds then stepped up to the man with a mumbled, "Excuse me, Sir." The wrapped rock in his hand made a muffled thud; the fellow slumped to the ground, a welt rising on the back of his head, and Féolan was over the barricade, sprinting for cover. He lay flat in a ditch, peering through a screen of shrubbery and rain, until he was sure that he had not been noticed. Then he got to his feet and ran as only an Elf can run, light and tireless, elated despite the danger to be free again under the night sky.

GABRIELLE WAS READY. It had been easy, in the end: She said no more to her father and simply prepared to go along. She had borrowed some clothes from Tristan so as to blend in better as the muster prepared to head out, but the king, busy with his own preparations, would pay little attention to the bonemenders trailing at the end of the procession along with the provisions and gear. There was a good chance she and her father would never cross paths during the entire journey.

Justine and the children were staying at Castle DesChênes, though they were prepared to retreat to the Island if need be. Gabrielle was glad. She had not felt right about leaving Solange to worry alone at home. Now at least Solange and Justine would have each other.

But Gabrielle still had an awkward conversation ahead of her. She had wavered for days about whether to tell her mother. Was it unfair to ask her to keep a secret from Jerome? What if her mother felt duty-bound to tell? Yet Gabrielle could not disappear without a word of explanation. And so, the morning before their departure, she asked Solange to walk with her to the back garden.

Sitting on the stone bench under the rose trellis, Gabrielle steeled herself to begin. But Solange did not wait for her careful speech.

"You are riding out with the army, aren't you?"

Gabrielle was amazed. "How did you know?"

Solange gave her a small, sad smile. "I guess I really am your mother. I know you, Gabrielle. When have you ever allowed convention, or even your father's authority, to govern your own conscience?"

Am I really that headstrong? Gabrielle wondered. She had always seen herself as a dutiful daughter. But when she believed her convictions really mattered, then yes, she was that headstrong.

"If you have such a compelling feeling that you must go, then I think you should," Solange continued. "But by all that's holy, be as careful as you can, Gabrielle. When I think of the danger … "

The two women embraced.

"Does Tristan know?" asked Solange, wiping her eyes.

"Yes."

"Good. You can keep watch on each other."

"I didn't know if I should tell you," confessed Gabrielle. "I didn't think I should ask you to keep a secret from Father."

"And so you shouldn't," said Solange tartly. Then, grinning, "But you'd be surprised what I've kept from Jerome over the years."

Gabrielle couldn't help laughing through her tears. There was certainly more to her mother than met the eye.

THE RAIN STOPPED just before dawn, and as the sun rose Féolan was through the foothills and heading into the first fingers of the mountains themselves. He was soaked through, hungry and sore from the "lessons" he'd been given—by fists and booted feet—before being locked up, but he meant to put as much distance as possible between himself and the *Gref Orisé* before stopping. The footing was treacherous, mud and half-melted snow slicked over rock, and he walked now, trotting over the firmer places. Impossible not to leave footprints in such ground, especially in his heavy military boots. If they followed him this far, they would know where he went. Would they bother? They might. Deserters would likely be hunted diligently as an example to the other men.

By late morning the sun was actually warm, and Féolan shucked off the wet cloak. He found a length of deadwood about right for a staff and slung the cloak over it, to dry as he walked. He hoped the sun would shine long enough to dry the clothes he was wearing too. With a pang of regret, he thought of the food and clothing he had stashed in his pack and then had to leave behind.

The sun had just edged past its zenith when he heard hoofbeats. Checking all paths, Féolan thought grimly. You had to hand it to the *Gref Orisé*; they were thorough. He glanced around, checking the site. Better, he concluded, to face them here than risk being overtaken in a cut with no cover. Climbing up the rock face on his left to a wide ledge, he hunkered down behind a large boulder. He would see who he was up against, then decide whether to fight or flee.

Two horsemen trotted into view, only partially armored with helmets and breastplates. One was extremely muddy, as was his horse. Neither looked happy. Bad footing for horses, Féolan mused. Only two men. How he wished for his bow!

One of the men swore under his breath and pointed to where Féolan's footprints suddenly ended. Both looked around uneasily.

"What in hellfire is he goin' this way for, anyhow?" burst out the muddy rider. "We ain't enough to take down a deserter! They send half a bloody regiment the other way, where he ain't, and only us two fer a 'precaution,' they says, up here. He must be some kinda maniac to be takin' the same bloody path as the army he's sneakin' away from!"

"Just shuddup and look sharp," snarled the other. At that moment Féolan made his decision. He sighted quickly, flicked his wrist and a second later his knife blade had buried itself in the back of the muddy soldier's arm. Féolan ducked down and set his back against the boulder, heaving it into the trail, then leaped lightly over the ledge. The scene was bedlam, the spooked horses rearing, the soldiers sawing at their reins and cursing. Darting in at his shield-arm side, Féolan dragged the second soldier to the ground and grappled for control of the sword. He could not prevail without it, but the man was strong and gripped onto his weapon like a limpet.

Féolan bucked up and came down with his knee raised, thrusting it hard into the little scallop in the breastplate that allowed a man to bend at the waist. It was a painful landing—the area was still protected by chain link mesh—but worse for his opponent. The wind whistled from the man's lungs in a rush, and in that moment Féolan dared to clap both hands to the sword-arm, give it a quick lift and twist, and bring it down hard, thumb first, on the rock below. He heard an agonized grunt, and the hand shuddered open. There was no time for nicety. Féolan snatched up the sword and ran the man through. He turned to face his remaining foe.

The soldier was pale with fear and confusion. Féolan's shaggy hair and rough clothing could no longer conceal the fact that this · was no cowardly runaway; his Elf's eyes blazed and he came on with complete confidence. Shaking his head frantically, the soldier dropped his sword and raised his arms in surrender. Féolan walked on until his sword was inches from the man's face.

"By rights I should kill thee," he said. "Yet perhaps your wound is enough to keep you from battle, and that serves my purpose well enough. I will spare thee, at least until you disobey my word."

Speechless, the soldier simply nodded.

"Drop your knife."

"I have none," blurted the soldier.

Féolan narrowed his eyes. "I will search it out with my sword if you cannot find it. Your knife."

"I have none, truly," the man insisted, his voice desperate. "I lost it in a game of tiles."

Féolan saw that the soldier spoke true. "Off your horse, then. You must walk."

Wincing from the knife-wound, the man slid awkwardly from his horse.

"Good. There is but one last thing, before you go. I must have my blade."

"Your ... " The soldier's eyes strayed to his right bicep, where the hilt of Féolan's knife hung. It angled toward the back, making it awkward for the soldier to grasp it himself.

"It is not a thing for the likes of you to possess," said Féolan. "If you will trust me, it will be better if I pull it."

"Trust you!" The soldier found his voice and managed an incredulous laugh. Yet as he searched Féolan's face, he must have found something, after all, to trust, for he gritted his teeth and presented his arm. Féolan pulled the knife as smoothly as he could, and sent the soldier stumbling down the road back to his garrison.

Now for the horses. The black seemed the calmer of the two, but something in the chestnut mare called to him. She was skittish now, but he sensed within her a more responsive heart.

The chestnut, then. Féolan stepped up to her softly. She back-stepped a little, rolling her eyes. He did not reach for the reins, or hinder her in any way, but spoke quietly in his own tongue. Reaching his mind out to hers, he offered friendship in place of the domination she had known. He stood before her, still and calm, and little by little she sidled up to him. Soon he felt her soft nose against him as she gingerly snuffled and blew against his clothes and hair. Still, he did not move or attempt to touch her. He let her see what he was: a friend. The ripply shivers up and down her hide slowed, then stopped; the nervous snorting relaxed. At last she laid her head against him, and he stroked her neck and velvet muzzle, murmuring gentle reassurances. Calmly he moved around her, stroking and talking. He unbuckled the heavy saddle, lifted it from her and laid it aside. The reins he left for now, hateful though they seemed to him; she would not yet understand his guidance and would feel more secure with them. The black's reins he took, cutting through one end to make a long thong that he tied to his belt. He hadn't time to gentle both now, and he couldn't let a horse return free yet.

He came back to the chestnut, laid his hand on her forehead, and asked her simply: Will you carry me? When he settled on her back, she tossed her head a bit at the unfamiliar feeling, then steadied. With the black in tow, they followed the twisting path leading into the clouds.

CHAPTER 17

THEIR departure was not how Gabrielle had pictured it. She had imagined the brave Verdeau troops, rank on rank, charging out of town at full gallop. And they had, eventually, marched out of town in ordered ranks, but only after a long, noisy, crowded gathering in the fields outside of the castle. The army was three thousand men strong, one-third on horseback, followed by endless carts of food, weaponry, medical and other supplies. It takes a very long time to get three thousand men all en route along a road wide enough for three horses, Gabrielle discovered. The bonemenders, among the last in line, stood in the field for over half the day before they finally got underway.

She had been right about the need for leadership. The bonemenders did not all consider themselves to be under military command. During the long wait, some became frustrated and angry, as if their time were being wasted deliberately. Some had decided to wander into town for a last pint while they waited. It was Gabrielle's diplomatic insistence that kept them in their places, ready to move out when their turn came.

They marched until dark, then set up their camps strung out along both sides of the road. Without the bottleneck effect they had experienced on first setting out, their departure the next morning was swift.

After three more days, traveling north on the River Road from dawn until dark, the army had passed Ratigouche and crossed over the border of La Maronne. By then Gabrielle, like everyone else, was weary and footsore. That evening she sent the bonemenders throughout the camp, treating blisters and pulled muscles, knowing these small complaints could lead to serious problems if ignored.

At Gaudette, the royal city of La Maronne, they learned that the bulk of the Maronnais army, some twenty-five hundred men, had marched out two days previous to take up position at the Eastern Gateway. On the sixth day they crossed the Smoky River, and Gabrielle felt a thrill of recognition. The Smoky, and Otter Lake beyond it, had been among the landmarks mentioned in Féolan's note. Foolish though it was, she couldn't shake the feeling that at any moment he might wander out of the woods and step onto the road before her eyes.

The land grew rough and the road narrower. They were entering the Maronnais highlands, leading up to the Krylian Mountains. Still, they made the approach to the pass before noon on the eighth day. The troops were given leave to rest where they were while Jerome and his general took stock of the terrain and developed their battle plan. Gabrielle and her bonemenders took shifts, leaving one on duty for the steady trickle of patients with blisters, sprains, cuts or colds. She forced herself to roll in a blanket and rest, though her instinct was to see to these men herself. She did leave word that any serious sprains should be sent to her for healing. Sprains could take days to resolve on their own, and the soldiers needed to be fit for active combat.

By suppertime, officers were making their way to all units, instructing them to set up camp behind the ridge of hills they were now sprawled along. Gabrielle braced herself. If she were to encounter Jerome, it would be now, as he toured the area to ensure the men were all placed as he wished. Instead, a happy surprise: Tristan himself appeared just as the last peg for the medic tent was hammered into place. Gabrielle was rummaging in a crate of medical supplies when she heard his voice. She stood, flipped back her long braid and grinned a welcome. "Come to have your blistered feet treated, my lord? Surely not, when you ride such a fine steed!"

"Blistered rear, more like," returned Tristan. He jumped off his horse and slung an arm around her shoulders. "How are you holding up, Gabi? Make the journey all right?"

"Fine, Tris. I'm fine." Gabrielle looked around her in mock despair. "It's going to take a while to get this set-up organized, though. It seems bonemenders aren't so skilled at pitching tents and lugging crates."

"We should have a couple of days, maybe more, before anything happens," he replied. "At least you've set up in the assigned place. That's better than some managed." The clinic area was at the back of the camp, beside the road. "Will this spot do, Gabi?" Tristan asked. "It's a bit of a ways to carry a wounded man, but you can't have the bonemenders trying to work in the midst of battle."

"I don't really know where we should be," Gabrielle confessed. "This seems as good a place as any." In truth, she couldn't picture an actual battle in her mind at all. Presumably, their soldiers would be positioned along the ridge, and the armies would engage in the valley below them. But it didn't seem real. Right now, the camp was full of purposeful bustle and the smell of cookfires, with no hint of an enemy anywhere. The scene felt more like a giant picnic than a prelude to war.

THE HEIGHTS OF the pass were treacherous, the rocky path buried in places by deep snow, rushing with snowmelt in others and buffeted by fierce winds always. Féolan had kept the black gelding with him overnight, then sent him home, but he still traveled with the chestnut mare. She had saved him travel time in the lower stretches, but these high narrow cuts were difficult for any horse, and their progress was slow. Still Arda—he had named her Arda—kept him warm on the coldest nights, trusted him to lead her along the most perilous paths and stood beside him, snorting defiance when the timber wolves howled their hunting song. He did not once consider leaving her behind. The generous heart he had sensed within her had blossomed day by day, and the ties of affection and loyalty between them were already strong.

For three days they struggled, picking their way around fallen boulders and sheets of ice slick with a layer of meltwater. Féolan grew gaunt with hunger, having subsisted only on the light rations he had found packed in his pursuers' saddlebags. Arda too had found little to eat in that bleak landscape. But late on the fourth day, he noticed that the walking was easier. Their way now sloped downhill. Sparse vegetation returned, and with it signs of animal life. That night, for the first time, the snares he set before sleeping caught a hare. By the end of the fifth day, he was able to ride most of the time. I may not be out of the mountains yet, but I'm out of the woods, he thought. Remembering his harrowing stay in *Gref Oris*, he was thankful to be returning in one piece.

He still had to decide where he was headed. Straight to Stonewater, to urge military action? Or was there time to find and alert the Humans first? Surely they would be moving into place by now, and he would find someone, if only a sentry force, at the entrance to the pass.

HE FOUND SOMEONE, all right. He found some very nervous sentries who almost shot him before he could identify himself.

"Hold!" he shouted as arrows whistled past his ears. He stooped low over Arda, realizing that only the murky light of dusk had kept him from death. Berating himself for wandering unprotected into a battle zone, he bellowed the names that would proclaim him a friend. "I seek King Jerome DesChênes' forces! I am a friend of the Verdeau people! I have news of the *Gref Orisé*!" Idiot. You're not in Verdeau, and they don't call them *Gref Orisé*, his mind babbled. What in eternal night was the Maronnais king's name? He couldn't remember.

It didn't matter. It was Jerome's own sentries who had spotted him. After some rather excited demands that he identify himself further, throw down his weapons and dismount from his horse, he found himself face to face with the Verdeau soldiers. Within an hour, having told the sentries all he knew, he was on his way again, galloping east toward the Smoky River.

CHAPTER 18

IT was a waiting game now: waiting for the runners to reach the Eastern Gateway and summon help; waiting for the Maronnais army to arrive; waiting for the Greffaires to strike. No main road led from the Eastern Gateway to their own location at the Skyway Pass, though shepherd paths and cart tracks did meander along the edge of the foothills. A couple of runners could make good speed through that country, if they did not mistake their way, but not a full army. It was difficult to guess what route their reinforcements would choose and how long they might take.

Tristan brought the news to the clinic station, bursting in with his usual lack of preamble. "Gabi, there's news! You won't believe it; it's from Féolan."

Gabrielle's face flushed red before she could stop it. That rushing in her ears when she heard his name—would it never stop?

Tristan noticed. "Damn the gods, Gabi, I'm sorry. I wasn't thinking…"

"Forget about it," said Gabrielle, overlooking his crude language as well. She had become used to far worse in recent days. "What's happened?"

Quickly Tristan filled her in.

"Do we have enough men?" she asked.

"Not if Féolan's numbers are right. Not unless the Maronnais get here in time. They've sent runners. You know," he went on, "I would think the mountains are just barely passable now. Féolan must have gone over there weeks ago. I wonder how he got through."

Gabrielle just shook her head. The Greffaires were coming. Now it was real.

The days passed. The men grew jumpy and tense; training drills were apt to erupt into angry scuffles. Tristan proved his worth ten times over in those days, keeping his men alert and focused while smoothing over the rough edges of tension. Gabrielle and her bonemenders fine-tuned their makeshift clinic, setting up a workspace well stocked with supplies for each bonemender and a waiting area for the injured. They prepared poultices that would need only to be steeped in hot water before use, and Gabrielle herself boiled up the precise mix of mandragora and henbane that would be used—poured onto a cloth and held over the patient's nostrils if he was unable to drink—to allay the pain of the most terrible wounds. She gathered together the military medics and reviewed their training. And then she too waited.

The runners returned, horses and riders stumbling with exhaustion. The Maronnais were coming, but they would be at least three more days. They would cross the Smoky River at the ford at Loutre and make their way up the main road from there.

IT WAS JUST PAST noon when the sentries flew into camp, and the alarms started blaring. The Greffaires were moving through the foothills, maybe an hour away, not much more. The Verdeau army prepared hurriedly, cookfires abandoned in a rush for helmets, weaponry and horses. They were massed on the ridge in orderly ranks, looking north into the wide valley General Fortin had chosen for the battle, before any sign of the enemy could be seen. Brave and bold they stood, row on row of silver helms and resolute faces. The sight stirred even Gabrielle's heart with wild hope. She and a few of the other noncombatants climbed a hill behind the ridge so that they too could gaze north, waiting for the first figures to appear on the other side.

The vista was beautiful, were they in a mood to see it. The valley spread out below them, open and green, between dark walls of forest. It narrowed to a finger on the far side where it swept up toward the mountains. And behind rose the dark Krylians, forested hills stacked like massed soldiers before the soaring, bare peaks of the highest summits.

When they came it was like a river spilling down the hillside and flooding the plain. The Verdeau men fell silent, the brave jokes and boasts dried up in their throats as the huge army spread out to face them. Gabrielle reminded herself that many of these Greffaires were untrained and unwilling serfs. Still, her heart sank. The sheer advantage of their numbers was crushing.

"They are three to our one," the mess boy beside her muttered. His face was gray with fear.

"Battles are not won by numbers alone. And the Maronnais ride to our aid," she told him. But she had to force the words out. This battle, she knew, would not be won.

A sudden, desperate thought came to her. She ran back to the clinic, rummaged in boxes until she found ink and a scrap of parchment, and scribbled a note. Then pulling a much-folded paper from her inside pocket, she thrust both in an empty medicine bag.

"Here, Pascal, is it? How would you like to get out of here and help Verdeau while you're at it? Can you read a map?" She pulled out Féolan's paper and went over the directions with the youth, who was all too happy to volunteer. Soon he was on one of the older horses that had been tethered behind the clinic tent. "Ask the villagers and shepherds to help you find the landmarks. When you are near the place, call out. There will be hidden sentries. Let them know whom you seek and from whom you are sent. All luck be with you." She smacked the horse on the rear, sending him cantering down the road.

IN FACT, THE Greffaire army had not expected to meet resistance this close to the border. Commander Col had been confident that his invasion would surprise the people of the Krylian Basin. He had not expected significant fighting before Gaudette; he had even allowed himself to hope they might advance into Verdeau before any sizeable force could be mustered against him. The first sight of the massed ranks gathered along the ridge, obviously well prepared and waiting, had given Col some unpleasant moments.

If General Fortin had known Col's thoughts, he would have also known that the Greffaire soldiers had not taken the precaution of donning their battle armor before entering enemy territory. But he was not sure, and he could not see past the thick ranks of the conscripts, who had been driven ahead of the regular troops right through the mountain pass. So, instead of calling for an immediate charge across the valley and striking while the Greffaire army was still in some confusion, he had waited, opting instead to make them come across to more favorable ground. He thus lost an important advantage, but he preserved the position of his archers, now hidden in the corridors of scrubby woodland that bordered the plain to east and west. And, perhaps more important, he kept open the line of retreat.

Looking across the valley as his troops scrambled to suit up for battle, Col decided that he had little to worry about, except perhaps the dark clouds massing along the eastern horizon. The opposing force was almost laughably small. Why, he had nearly as many conscripts as their entire army! And he did not think he was mistaken that their warriors were poorly protected: he could make out helmets, but the mid-day sun would have glinted off full armor. They would be no match for his full-suited elite. Col grinned. It would be good for the men to taste victory so early in the campaign.

THE STONEWATER COUNCIL had been disturbed enough by Féolan's description of the *Gref Orisé* regime to call together a Council of Elders. Féolan chafed against the delay, but knew this was the only way to effect a full-scale Elvish resistance. His own community was too small to mount a significant force.

It was only days, though it seemed like weeks, before he found himself addressing the leaders of the Elvish people, many unknown to him, all at least a century his senior. He knew that his youth, not to mention the impulsive foolishness of his foray across the mountains, hardly recommended him. Still, many in the room held personal memories of the last *Gref Orisé* invasion, and though they might not be anxious to repeat the losses of that struggle, they ought at least to recognize the truth of his story.

In detail, he laid out what he had seen and heard. His conclusion was passionate: "I cannot describe to you the oppression endured by these people. Even their own citizens know no freedom. If the *Gref Orisé* prevail in this land, never again will we wander at will across the countryside. Our settlements are secret now because we wish it so—but they will become secret of necessity, for our very survival. If we become known, we will be hunted. We will be prisoners in our own homeland."

The silence dragged on as the Elders considered his words. Féolan stood patiently, knowing this could not be rushed. At last there followed several clarifying questions of a tactical nature—details of the *Gref Orisé* weaponry, fighting style, body armor—which encouraged Féolan hugely. Finally, a senior Elder, her eyes deep wells of age, rose to speak.

"It appears to me," she said, "that we would be most effective striking at this army not on the battlefield but while they are en route or encamped, hitting suddenly and by surprise and then fading away. That uses our strengths against their weaknesses, does it not? I do not discount that there might also arise a reason to join our force of arms with the Humans in a direct encounter, but as a general strategy we might hamper their progress significantly through progressive ambushes. What think you, Féolan?"

Startled at being asked a further opinion, Féolan gathered his thoughts. "One thing I did not mention is that *Gref Oris*—at least the part I saw—is an open country, full of wide plains and few trees. They are unused to woodlands. I suspect this type of warfare is unknown to them."

The atmosphere in the room sharpened as many unspoken thoughts were exchanged. The Council was moving toward a decision.

Another spoke. "The Humans oppose these *Gref Orisé* already. They may succeed. Why not watch their progress and stand ready to send our own people should they falter?"

Féolan could not keep silent. "Will we send the Humans to die on our behalf?" he demanded. "Does the short season of their lives make them worth less than our own? This seems to me a shameful proposal."

The head of Féolan's own Council, Tilumar, narrowed his eyes.

"Forgive me," Féolan muttered. "It was not my place to speak so." But the tall, ancient Elf who had spoken rose to his feet.

"You speak true," he said. "And I speak from my own loss rather than from the wisdom that befits one of my years. Many of my people died in the last war. But that is, in the end, a poor reason to stand aside so others may die as well."

Féolan, who had never known the untimely death of kin or friend, was humbled by this Elf's honesty. But before anyone could speak a messenger was admitted.

"I apologize for interrupting the Council's business," he began. "But an envoy has arrived from the Verdeau army, and I thought his news might have bearing on your deliberations. It is addressed to Féolan of Stonewater."

Heart pounding, Féolan took the crumpled scrap of parchment. His eyes flew to the signature at the bottom of the brief note. At Tilumar's prompting, he forced himself to raise his voice and read aloud:

> Féolan,
> We face battle at the Skyway Pass. Desperately out-
> numbered. If there is help to be had from your people, I
> beg it now. If not, yet do I send my love.
> Gabrielle.

Desperate now to be on his way, Féolan crossed swiftly to Tilumar and sank to his knees. Ignoring the mild shock in the room, he spoke quietly to his Elder, without pride or defiance. "Tilumar. I have told you how this woman saved Danaïs from the brink of death and how her family welcomed us as royal guests. That alone puts on me at least a bond of obligation. I have not told how Gabrielle and I came to love one another. I am bound to aid her if I can."

Tilumar studied him. "Well, Féolan," he said, "you astonish me. Yet ever you have followed your own path. Ride to battle if you must, with my blessing."

But Féolan was not finished. "I will ride alone, if needs be. But little will one warrior avail anything. Tilumar, I know there is no time for a concerted effort. Probably anything we send will be too late. But since there is at least some agreement in the room that this war concerns the Elves as well, I beg leave to take a force from Stonewater now, in hope the defense may yet be bolstered."

Tilumar frowned. "Stonewater is close to the invasion's path. Our own home must remain strongly defended." Féolan kept silence as Tilumar thought. "You may take ten units. It is not enough to turn the tide of battle. Aim for a strategic target, as we discussed. I do not want our people engaging in direct warfare until the Council has made its decision."

Ten dozen men. Springing to his feet, Féolan thanked Tilumar and, hand on breast, bowed to the Council. As he headed for the door, Tilumar stopped him.

"Féolan. You are not to waste Elvish lives in futile heroics. Not even for your Lady."

"I understand, my Lord."

CHAPTER 19

THE armies met in the first clash of battle, and once again General Col was surprised by the turn of events. As he drove his conscripts down to meet the enemy, a number of them bolted into the woodlands bordering the battlefield. Enemy troops made no attempt to pursue them, and soon conscripts at each edge of his formation were streaming into the woods. Col lost a couple of hundred before he sent his own soldiers hurrying down to cut them off. Later, in the midst of heated fighting—and few though they were, he had to acknowledge that he faced trained, tough-minded men—empty corridors would mysteriously appear in the defense, allowing the conscripts to penetrate unhindered deep into enemy lines. But the untrained and unmotivated conscripts did not take advantage of their position. They simply pushed right through and ran away. In this way at least five hundred conscripts were wasted.

The second surprise involved the archers, who were hidden in the very woods into which the conscripts had escaped. They held their fire through the first advance, saving their arrows for the trained soldiers who came in the second wave. Even the elite, heavily armored soldiers, if they were close to the archers' ranks, were often pierced by the heavy shafts, which were deadly to the less protected soldiers throughout the field. When Col tried to charge these archers, they melted back into the woods faster than his men, in their heavy suits, could follow.

As the afternoon wore on, hand-to-hand fighting raged over the field. Col's regular army was fully engaged now, and while the enemy was showing fatigue from dealing with the first wave of conscripts, his own men were unsettled by the rain of arrows through which they had been forced to advance. Then too the Basin men's style of fighting was so very different from their own that it was difficult to tell who had the advantage. Col's men were far better protected (though many of the enemy did wear light chain mail), but they could not match the speed and agility of their foes. So while the enemy was hard-pressed to injure the Greffaires, so were the Greffaires, especially once they became tired themselves, hard-pressed to strike the Basin soldiers.

Dark came early and with it a violent storm that turned the battlefield into a black chaos. The horns to retreat sounded almost simultaneously from the two sides, and both armies made camp, to take some uneasy rest and await the dawn.

Col ate his cold supper stonily. This day had displeased him. On the morrow his force of numbers must prevail, but there had been too many losses. Too many surprises. These men of the Basin—they had known of his coming. Would such armies await him all the way to the sea? He sighed, and then, tired though he was, rose to tally losses and review the next day's plans with his regiment commanders. His only son, Derkh, was in Fourth Regiment, and Col's last act of the night was to check that he was unharmed. Finally, the feared commander returned to his tent, stripped off his wet clothes and slept.

GABRIELLE DID NOT sleep; nor did her bonemenders, save in short, exhausted snatches. All that long afternoon the dying and wounded had filled the clinic tents; then as the fighting stopped and rescue efforts began in earnest, the river of patients became a flood. The bonemenders worked at fever pitch as the air filled with the groans and cries of injured men, all now soaked and chilled from the flash storm. Gabrielle could use her healing power only for the most desperate of cases; while she bent in her trance over one man, three more might die waiting. As for her precious mandragora mixture, it was used mostly to ease the pain of those doomed to die and for surgery; its safe use required such careful monitoring that they simply couldn't spare the time.

Tristan's sudden appearance was the only bright spot in that terrible night. He was muddy, visibly tired and nearly as bloodstained as Gabrielle herself, but his irrepressible spirits seemed untouched. She had never been so relieved to see anyone.

"Did you see any of the battle, Gabi?" he asked.

"No, Tristan." Gabrielle tried to keep the impatience out of her voice. "I wasn't able to get away."

"I didn't mean it would be fun to watch," he protested. "I just meant that you would have been so proud of our men. It's one thing to practice fighting, you know, and another when it's the real thing. Our men proved their worth today."

"I hear your men would face the Dark One himself for you, Tris," said Gabrielle.

"Well," he said modestly. "It wasn't just us. But we did devise a way to get past those tin suits. You have to do it with two men. One engages the enemy head-on and keeps him busy, while the other circles around and darts in, slicing at the straps and stabbing through the little joint-openings. A whole bunch of other units picked up that little trick from us."

A horn sounded, two long notes and two short. "I have to go," said Tristan. "Be careful tomorrow, Gabi. There's talk of a retreat. Be ready to get out of here fast."

Late that night word came that the injured were to be moved out. Despite the brave day's battle, Fortin knew that the Greffaire force was too large to be defeated without help. Unless reinforcements arrived, he would call a retreat on the morrow. All who could walk or be moved on a cart were to head south now toward Gaudette, accompanied by some of the bonemenders. With any luck, they would get far enough away to avoid a Greffaire pursuit.

Wearily, Gabrielle assigned five bonemenders to make the journey and helped move the patients to the crude carts. The trip would be exhausting and painful for all of them but preferable no doubt to being overrun by the enemy. She wondered grimly how many would die on the road.

"Why don't you go along with them, Lady Gabrielle?" It was Manon, a bonemender from Ratigouche. "You've done so much already, and you might keep some of these poor souls alive."

How she would love to. She had seen enough suffering and death this day to last her a lifetime: she could barely force herself to return to the clinic tent with its thick stench of blood and fear and pain.

But she had to. Whatever she had come here for, it hadn't happened yet.

THE HORNS SOUNDED at dawn, and by mid-morning General Fortin had made his decision. The tide was turning against them.

The men were becoming exhausted and exhaustion benefited the armored Greffaires. It was time for a retreat. Somewhere to the south, they would join up with the Maronnais army and find a new place to make a stand.

Cook tents and supply wagons had been sent down the road early that morning. Now horns all over the field sent the troops after them—all but a mounted rear guard who would try to hold the Greffaires at bay while the bulk of the army made as much distance as possible.

It was an orderly process, as retreats go, but to the bonemenders it looked like utter confusion, with men streaming by from all directions. A commander pounded by on horseback. "Get going!" he shouted at them. "It's a retreat! Grab your gear and get out of here!"

Shaken out of her bemusement, Gabrielle shoved precious medical supplies into packs. She shouted at the bonemenders to get the bigger crates and the remaining patients into the last carts lumbering by. One young man was dying, but she could not bring herself to leave him behind. She and the bonemenders grabbed their cloaks and hurried toward the road.

Swept into the anxious mass of men fleeing south, Gabrielle stiffened. Panic froze her features. She turned and began struggling back against the relentless tide of men. She had to get to the battlefield. She had to. Someone she loved was hurt.

CHAPTER 20

ALL her fear had been for Tristan, but it was her father she found. He lay on the ground behind a knot of Verdeau soldiers. Though they fought ferociously to protect their king, they fought with little hope. As the rear guard fell back, too beset even to notice that Jerome had fallen, the king's guard was stranded on the field. Soon they would be overrun.

Ignoring the roar of battle and the litter of corpses around her, Gabrielle dodged through the screen of soldiers, dropped to her knees and cradled Jerome in her lap. She could not, at first, see where he was injured. The ground was stained red about him, and his breath came in rasping gasps. She laid her hand along his neck. At her touch, his eyelids fluttered open.

"My Gabrielle," he whispered. "Do I dream?"

"Shhhh," she soothed, stroking his brow. She could not have managed words, so close were her tears.

"You must go," Jerome said, each word a painful effort. "Go."

Gabrielle rested her hand on Jerome's forehead, closed her eyes and sank into him. As her vision shifted, she could find nothing at first. Heart, lungs, limbs—all were fine. Wait. Something funny about his legs. What was it? They seemed...whole, but dead. No, that made no sense. She continued on...and then she saw it, and her heart sank. Jerome had been struck in the back—by a battle-ax, she guessed. The powerful blow had all but severed his spine.

Despair welled up in her. Gabrielle saw all too clearly her father's fate if he were taken off the field now. The move would be almost bound to kill him. If by some chance he lived, it would be to face paralysis, organ failure, an early wasting death. It was unthinkable. Now, before the fragile nerves of the spinal cord began to deteriorate, she must reattach them. She could do it. Was it not for this she had been sent here? She would do it, and if any of his men still lived, they would carry him to safety.

Never had her concentration been so fierce. The fury around her vanished; her own body vanished; even Jerome himself was only vaguely in her consciousness. Nothing existed for her but the intricate repair of the delicate hair-thin shafts, the healing light that shone through and over the tissues, the power pulsing through her hands. An hour crawled by, and miraculously the king's guard held, and she worked undisturbed. The repairs were fragile yet, but they were true—she could feel the energy pulsing through the newly joined fibers. If she could just finish all the initial joins and then firm up the cracked spine, she would risk moving him.

She did not hear the final call to retreat. The soldiers did, but by then their avenue of escape had long been cut off. One of Jerome's men shook her shoulder and yelled for her to make haste and run. Gabrielle's eyes snapped open, blazing with such fire that he flinched from their heat. "I cannot leave him!" she snarled, shaking off the soldier's hand, and sank back into her work. So motionless was Gabrielle, so deeply bent over her father's body, that while one by one the king's guards were slaughtered, the swarming Greffaire soldiers took no more notice of her than of the corpses under their feet.

One noticed Jerome, though. Having joined in the pursuit of the retreating rear guard, and then been recalled by the horns cutting short the chase, a Greffaire soldier trudged across the field with his company. He was more than glad to disengage; his armor was damnably hot and his arse ached from a horse kick. He swung his sword as he walked, looking forward to a long drink and a well-heaped plate. A shock of reddish hair and a gleam of white throat caught his eye. As casually as a boy kicking a stone, he swung the sword high and brought it down through the exposed neck. Stepping over the head that rolled at his feet, he continued his stolid walk.

CHAPTER 21

GABRIELLE'S body went rigid. Where was he? She groped with her mind. Where was he? Jerome had been present with her, his spine healing under her hand, his heart beating in concert with her own, and then there was just ... silence.

Gabrielle jerked out of her trance with a violence that left her gasping and dazed. She felt pain and saw with dull indifference that her own thigh was bleeding from a shallow slice just above the knee. The terrible body in her arms was beyond her; her mind simply refused to see it. First came a growing sense of dread so dark she felt it would smother her. She ground her teeth and whimpered from the effort not to know. That head, that gray face and staring eye, that was not, could not be, her father.

Then her eye caught a glint of copper—an earring, small and wide, chased with engraving, and she could pretend no longer. The memory rose within her, tearing at her heart: her father young and brawny, opening Solange's birthday gift and protesting, "But I don't have a pierced ear!"

"I have always thought you would look very handsome with one," Solange had replied, and they had laughed and kissed, while little Tristan tried to climb up their legs. Now Jerome was beyond the skill of any healer from earth or sky. He was dead.

A terrible groan clawed its way out of her. You didn't save him, a cold voice accused. She could not answer it. She could only hold on to what was left of him and cry out in anguish for the man who had made her his daughter.

GABRIELLE BARELY FELT the hard grip of the soldier who hauled her off her father's body and set her on her feet, though he left a set of deep bruises in the flesh of her arm. Dazed with grief, she peered at the man through swollen eyelids. Only slowly did she understand her situation: she was an unprotected woman on an enemy field. She was booty. With a jolt of fear, Gabrielle looked more closely at the ring of men surrounding her. Her fate was as clear as the wolfish hunger on their faces. There was nowhere to run.

Better to have fallen under a sword than this. They were tight around her now, more falling in behind and jostling those in front. She heard a voice raised in blustery threat—the man who first found her. Defending his claim, she thought bitterly.

Gabrielle was shoved hard from behind and stumbled forward into the soldiers. Hands grabbed and pulled at her, then she was pushed again. Someone tripped her as she staggered off balance, and she fell to a burst of rough laughter. It was a sound so predatory it turned her belly to ice. Her mouth filled with the taste of brass. The taste of fear.

A harsh shout and the crack of a whip rang through the air. Gabrielle flinched, but the whip was not for her. A soldier on horseback harangued the men angrily. Gabrielle thought she caught the word "commander," but in her terror she understood little else of the thick dialect. Muttering sullenly, the soldiers backed away. Tossing his horse's reins to a nearby soldier, the officer dismounted, dragged Gabrielle up by the arm and strode across the field.

Gabrielle struggled to keep up. She knew only one thing: It was better to be at the mercy of one man than ten. They stopped at last before a tent with a posted guard. Gabrielle guessed she was to be presented to the commander.

He was powerfully built, nearly bald, forceful in his manner. He did not seem pleased at the interruption.

"What do I want with this?" he snapped. "Do you suppose I am in the mood for a woman now?"

It took all Gabrielle's concentration to follow their conversation, but the language was similar enough to her own to catch the meaning.

"I'm sorry, Commander Col," her rescuer said. "I thought it best to enforce the rule, nevertheless."

There was a silence. "You're right," Col replied. He ran a hand over his smooth head. "Leave her here." His eyes swept her up and down. She forced herself to stand straight, defiant. "She's a bloody mess. Can't even tell if she's worth the bother."

Col dismissed the soldier and pointed to the far corner of the tent. "Sit down there. Do you understand me?"

"Yes, sir. I understand some," said Gabrielle, hating the quaver in her voice. She slumped to the ground.

"Tired?" Col said, his manner indifferent. "It's a tiring business." He lowered himself onto a low stool, crossed his arms and studied her more closely. "You look like you've been swimming in blood," he said. "Take those dirty clothes off; it would be a big improvement."

In the silence that followed, Gabrielle did her best to become invisible, but the commander's interest in her had been kindled.

He jumped to his feet. "Ah, maybe the good captain was right. Take my mind off the boy." He reached for Gabrielle's wrist. "C'mere, you."

Gabrielle stiffened and shrank from his touch. "I am a bonemender!" she heard herself babble. "You cannot violate a bonemender!" What pathetic nonsense, she thought. This man wouldn't care if I were the Spirit of the Gray Sea herself.

Strangely enough, though, Col hesitated. He looked at her sharply.

"Bonemender." He didn't seem to know the word. "You are a ... surgeon?"

"I help sick and wounded people get better. If that's a surgeon, then yes."

A shadow darkened the man's hard face. Some deep pain was hidden here. "Are you any good?" he demanded.

It was hardly the time for false modesty. "Better than most," she said.

"My son is dying," he said. "My surgeons can do nothing for him. You want to save yourself? Save him." He headed out the door. "Come," he ordered.

COL THRUST HER INSIDE the tent. A slight figure lay hunched on a pallet against the wall. Gabrielle had not expected this: Col's son was so young, no more than fourteen or fifteen, she judged. A bracing flame of anger licked at her: The brute, to send his own boy into battle! The boy stared at her, frightened eyes huge in a white face.

"Are you the Angel of Death?" he whispered. She realized suddenly how sinister she must look, so filthy and disheveled, and smiled in spite of herself.

"No, no," she said softly. She did not know if he would understand her speech. "I'm here to help you." She gestured at Col, asking him to explain. While he did, she knelt beside the boy—Derkh, his name was—and did a more careful appraisal. It was an abdominal wound, covered with a greasy bundle of bandaging, soaking red even now. The boy's skin was ghostly pale, his dark eyes hectic. She touched the back of her hand to his forehead and neck, no apparent fever yet, at least. His hands were pale and cold; he had lost a great deal of blood. A groan escaped him; he clamped his lips together hard but could not stifle the little mewing grunts that ended each breath. He was in terrible pain, Gabrielle realized, and struggling fiercely to be brave in front of his father.

Until this moment Gabrielle had not thought she would treat Col's son. She had imagined herself refusing boldly and going bravely to her death. Now the healer in her asserted itself. She had sworn to relieve suffering. This boy suffered; looking on him now she knew that nothing else mattered. He was not her enemy. He was her patient. She did not know if she had the skill and power left to help him, but she meant to try.

"I'll need boiling water, lots of it. Clean bandaging, not these dirty rags. I need healing herbs from my kit. It's on the battlefield where I was found." Gabrielle's tone was as clipped and commanding as if she were addressing a servant. Col raised an eyebrow but did not strike or rebuke her. He went to the door of the tent, rattled out a string of orders and turned back to her.

"What else?"

"I need to wash."

He grunted. "Don't we all?"

"I need to wash before I treat your son," she persisted. "Any dirt that gets in a wound can cause infection. In an abdominal wound, that could kill him."

Col yelled through the tent door again, and a bucket was brought in. As Gabrielle rose to her feet, a wave of dizziness washed over her and her vision blurred. She bent over her knees, fighting the faintness.

"What is it?" Col's voice was sharp. "Are you sick?"

"No," Gabrielle said. "But I do not remember when I last ate or slept."

"You can have water now. Food tonight, if my son is improved."

Col spoke again to the guard outside the tent and left without a backward glance.

WHEN THE SUPPLIES arrived, Gabrielle was already at work. The sword had thrust up under the boy's ribs, damaging the liver, and he was losing blood rapidly. Gabrielle's first priority was to seal the largest of the cut blood vessels. There was no prospect of reattaching them; she just hoped Derkh's body would be able to compensate for the blocked passages.

Before looking at the wound itself, she brewed up a light dose of the mandragora, mixed with a milder, and safer, willowbark mixture. It was the strongest painkiller she dared give the boy. Patiently she coaxed it into him, one small spoonful at a time. He gagged once or twice but fought it down, desperate for some relief. As the tea took effect, he closed his eyes.

"Derkh," she said, choosing the simplest words she could find. "It will hurt when I change the bandage. But the tea will help, and you will sleep after." He nodded; nobody needed to tell him that Gabrielle was his last hope.

The injury was ugly, all right; but Gabrielle was relieved to find a fairly clean layer of cloth next to the skin. She had been afraid the filth of the bandage alone would kill him. Derkh groaned and clenched his teeth as she began to rinse out the wound. "Cry out if you need to," she said, working as gently as she could. "Your father is not here, and I will not think the less of you. I've seen many a grown man show less courage than you." He must have understood at least some, for the rigid tension in his body eased a little, and though he did cry out—and cry—at the worst parts, he seemed calmer and less afraid. As promised, he dropped into a deep, exhausted sleep as she finished up the bandaging.

A man brought soup, cheese and a chunk of coarse bread, and Gabrielle made herself eat every scrap. Then she sat by Derkh's rough pallet and worked over him far into the night, until fatigue overcame her and she too collapsed into uneasy sleep.

CHAPTER 22

FOR two days the Greffaire forces camped just far enough away from the battlefield to be free of its stench. The official reason for the delay—and it made perfect sense to Col's troops—was to allow the men to scavenge valuable arms and armor from the dead of both sides. The true reason, which Col confessed to no one, was to give his son a chance to live. The strange "bonemender" had somehow pulled Derkh through that first night, when his own surgeons had left him for the dark road. Now she and his son would both have a second chance.

While the Greffaires tarried, La Maronne was on the move. The Verdeau troops, down to about twenty-five hundred men, marched southward toward Gaudette. Two thousand Maronnais, supported by some eight hundred soldiers from Gamier, marched west from the Eastern Gateway to meet them. Envoys galloped for Gaudette to request reinforcements from the castle garrison. And traveling faster than any of them, loping almost silently along secret forest pathways known only to the Elves, Féolan and his Stonewater warriors closed in on the Skyway Pass.

They found the battlefield easily. A valley strewn with death soon attracts clouds of carrion birds. Screened by the flanking woodlands, the Elves watched with disgust as *Gref Orisé* soldiers stripped the bodies of the fallen. Too late, thought Féolan. It is already lost.

But his military commander, Haldoryn, pointed out that there were too few bodies for a total defeat. "The losses were not all on the Verdeau side," said Haldoryn. "They gather plenty of their own armor. Plus if what you say about the use of conscripts is true, those poor souls must number many of the dead."

"So there was a retreat," concluded Féolan. "A retreat, perhaps, to join with fresh troops."

"That is my hope," agreed Haldoryn. "A retreat to buy time."

"Can we help to buy them that time?" asked Féolan.

Haldoryn thought, curling his lip in distaste at the sight of a soldier hacking a gold wristband from a dead soldier. "I have no taste for killing sleeping men unawares," he confessed. "But after looking upon this desolation, I believe I could stand it. I suggest we scout out the *Gref Orisé* camp."

GABRIELLE SPENT THOSE two days in Derkh's tent. The two guards posted outside were hardly necessary; she had no desire to take her chances among the Greffaire soldiers. Besides, in the deep healing trance she found a little oasis of oblivion, a respite from the pain of Jerome's death. Several times a day she changed Derkh's bandage and poultice and coaxed soups and medicines into him. The rest of the time she left the world and poured her mind into his healing, working until sleep pulled her down into blackness.

The first morning she had awakened on the ground beside Derkh's pallet, aching and chilled. She grimaced as she rose to her feet; her clothing was stiff with dried blood and gave off an acrid, meaty smell. Her thigh, where the sword had glanced off it, had bled and stuck to her skirt; the wound throbbed. Ironic, she thought, if she healed this half-dead boy, only to die herself from an infected flesh wound. She gave her leg a hasty wash, sprinkled dried goldenseal directly on the cut and covered it with what little bandaging she could spare. Then she turned to her patient.

He was watching her. His eyes looked better this morning, she saw with relief, clear and lucid.

"Your clothes smell awful," he said. Gabrielle nodded.

"Why don't you change them?"

"I have no others."

Derkh considered this while Gabrielle prepared new medicine for him. She could see the pain was starting to bite again.

"You can have some of mine," he announced as she tipped his head up to spoon in the tea.

Gabrielle hesitated. "Your father might not…"

"If my father is displeased, let him beat me," Derkh replied harshly. "It is my order. They are in that carryall. Take whatever is least dirty." He motioned with his chin.

Gabrielle took the top suit of clothes—a kind of tunic and strange, wide-cut pants. They were none too clean, but she wasn't about to paw through her captor's possessions. Derkh closed his eyes while she changed; the tang of young man's sweat enfolded her as she pulled the tunic over her head, and even so she was grateful for the improvement. There was a strange intimacy to wearing someone else's clothing.

Gabrielle gathered up her old skirt and overdress and looked at Derkh.

"Just throw them outside; someone will get rid of them."

She went to the door and paused.

"What is it?" asked Derkh.

"Nothing," said Gabrielle softly. "It's just… my father's blood is on them." The confession came out before she could stop it.

Derkh seemed taken aback. Maybe, like her, he hadn't really considered that grief and loss came to enemies as well as friends.

By the morning of the second day, Gabrielle knew that Derkh was out of danger. She was glad, for a bond of trust and respect had grown between them. She herself, however, was dangerously close to collapse. She didn't much care; exhaustion and heartsickness had taken too heavy a toll. But it occurred to her that with Derkh stable, she could slow her efforts to a more normal pace, and this might also buy the Basin troops the time they needed to regroup. Col had delayed this long for his son. Would he wait longer?

She attended to Derkh diligently that day but paced herself. Col checked on them around noon, and though he quickly regained his stern manner he could not suppress his surprised relief at finding Derkh resting comfortably, sipping at some broth.

"He will live?" he asked bluntly.

Gabriel nodded. "With rest and careful attention to his wounds, yes. He will live."

"Lucky for us both," he remarked. It was as close as he would come to thanking her.

CHAPTER 23

T HAT night, about a mile from camp, Haldoryn briefed his men one last time. "Get in and get out," he said. "No foolish risks. We want to disorient the enemy, put them on the defensive. We cannot make a serious dent in their numbers, but we can perhaps shake their confidence. Keep silence, stay cloaked in darkness. We rendezvous on this path, back where it crosses the stream."

"One more thing," added Féolan. "Some of these men are conscripts who fight against their will. They will be quartered together. Do not harm them, unless forced to it."

Except for the conscripts' compound, the *Gref Orisé* camp was not heavily guarded. No alarm sounded as the swift shadows flowed over the perimeter and vanished among the tents. Orange tongues of flame licked at the darkness: supply carts, ale barrels and cook tents sprang alight. A cry of "Fire!" rang through the camp as the startled sentries rushed to quench the flames. Two men drowsily guarding a large tent sprang to arms but too late; they died without a sound under the knives of two grim-faced Elves. Men thick with sleep poured from their tents with confused shouts; many were dead before their companions knew what had happened.

Commander Col did not rush out. He yelled for his guards, and when they did not appear, he strapped on his cuirass and helmet before cutting a strip out the back of the tent with his sword and stepping through.

Danaïs wiped his dagger and faded back into the shadow of a tree. He glanced at Féolan, his lips thin with disgust. "This is an ill night's work, my friend," he murmured.

"Aye," agreed Féolan. "Rather would I face a man full-armored and ready than kill from behind like a thief."

Danaïs stiffened. "It seems we get our wish," he said.

Féolan turned to the armored figure stalking toward them. He smiled ruefully. "At last I get to show off my *Gref Orisé* training," he said. "Danaïs, stay back, I beg you, and protect both our backs."

Féolan lowered his sword in the classic *Gref Orisé* fighting stance. Let him puzzle on that, he thought. The figure paused, then accepted his challenge. The duel began, unnoticed in the uproar all around them.

The man was a powerful and canny fighter, though against Féolan he seemed lumberingly slow. Féolan began two-handed, in the heavy slicing *Gref Orisé* style. As he got a feel for his opponent's moves, he switched to the more complex one-handed swordplay of his own people. He managed several nicks at the man's bare arms, and took a glancing blow on his fingers in return, but knew there could be no victory unless he penetrated the armor. Working his way toward his opponent's left side, he feinted and then leaped in with a powerful two-handed broadside sweep behind the man's knees. He was down. Danaïs leaped in, pinning the sword arm and sending the sword skidding across the bare ground while Féolan fell on the man's back, slit the armor laces and flicked open the clasps at the back of his helmet. The thick neck and shoulders lay exposed.

Féolan paused, breathing heavily. He should kill this man, his enemy, conquered in a fair fight. But his gorge rose at the thought of thrusting a sword into that unprotected neck. He pulled off the backplate, cast it aside and said, "Sit up, you."

His opponent sat warily, the breastplate falling away to reveal his chest still heaving with exertion.

"Now your helmet."

Féolan recognized the man immediately. He had seen him only once, but a striking presence like that was hard to forget.

"Good evening, Commander Col," he said. His sword stayed firmly trained at the man's neck.

Col swallowed his shock well. "How do you know my name?" he grated.

"I served in Unit Eighty-Six," replied Féolan. "And now, I think, there is no more time for talk. Pick up your sword, Commander, and fight me on even terms." He was well aware of Danaïs' alarm at this gesture, but he had no choice. He could not walk away, leaving the commander of the *Gref Orisé* forces alive and well, and he could not kill the man in cold blood. He would have to fight. And he would have to make a quick job of it, before they were noticed and men rallied to Col's aid.

It was almost easy. It had been many, many years since Col had fought without armor, and he left his side unprotected once too often. Leading with a quick feint, Féolan darted in and planted his sword deep between Col's ribs.

They did not wait to see the outcome. He and Danaïs slipped away, making for the woods east of camp.

GABRIELLE STARTED AWAKE to hammering footsteps, shouting and the crackle of fire. She leaped to her feet and peered out the doorway of the tent. It was a scene from a disjointed nightmare: the air full of smoke and shouting, the dark figures of running men glimpsed by the crazy flicker of flame. Her guards were gone.

An idea whispered in her: escape. Behind that a sudden longing: home.

She pulled back from the door, trying to order her thoughts.

"If you have a chance to go, take it."

Derkh's voice made her jump. She turned to him. "Take it," he insisted. "You have more than earned your freedom."

She crept over to his pallet. "I need to know that you will be well."

"I will," he replied. "I'm getting better now. You know it."

"You are, but as long as that wound is open it can get infected. Your ... uh, surgeons, they have to take care of it properly."

"Tell me how."

She did. She told him how to keep the wound clean: to insist on handwashing, boiled bandages and frequent dressing changes. She left behind the last of her poultice ingredients and told him how to dry and reuse them when he ran out. She gave him the names of the plants involved, in case his own surgeons kept a supply. And then she surprised herself by leaning over and kissing him on both cheeks. He reached up around her neck and pulled her close, and she was glad to feel the strength in his arms. Then she cracked open the tent flap and slid out into the orange and black night.

THERE WAS NO TELLING which way was best. Gabrielle hadn't even the sketchiest sense of the camp's layout; she just picked a direction and ran. Lacking the energy to dodge and hide, she blundered past the fighting and the fires, finding herself at last in the relative shelter of a stand of trees. Heaving for breath, legs trembling, she tried to catch her bearings. She had rarely been in the woods at night, but she found after a few minutes that she could pick out the blacker lines of the trees well enough. Cautiously, she made her way deeper into the brush, feeling for the ground beneath her feet, gaining confidence with each step. Gradually the clamor died away, until for the first time in many days she heard nothing but the soft sounds of nature. Moonlight outlined the birch trees with silver; an owl hooted. Her feet found a narrow path and followed it easily. She was not afraid.

Not, at least, until she heard voices up ahead. Gabrielle froze, her first dismayed thought that she had somehow circled around and blundered back to the Greffaire camp. Then she heard it again, not the harsh shouts of Greffaire soldiers but low, liquid voices speaking in a language like soft music. Her heart gave a lurch of recognition: they were Elves. They would help her. She had to catch up.

She was nearly there, all but running up the path, when she was tackled from behind. She fell, hard. Strong arms pinned her; she felt the tip of a knife or sword blade in her side. "Please! I am a friend!" she cried, unknowingly echoing Féolan's cry to the Verdeau guards. Then it seemed the thread of will that had brought her this far snapped; she fell silent and lay still. So be it, she thought. Better, at least, to die here under the trees than in that wretched camp. But her assailant was turning her over. Startled luminous eyes gazed at her, then widened in confusion. He sat her up, brushed her off, helped her to her feet, a stream of Elvish washing over her the while. Finally, standing unsteadily, Gabrielle realized he was asking a question.

"I'm sorry," she said, and her voice came out so shaky she had to swallow and start over. "I'm sorry. I don't speak Elvish."

THREE ELVES CAME slowly up the trail to the rendezvous point. One had taken a bad slash above the knee, and the other two supported him on either side. Féolan was well satisfied; as far as he could tell there had been no Elves lost and only one injury worse than this leg wound. They would do a more careful count once they were deeper into the woods.

The wounded man leaned heavily on Féolan as they worked their way up a steep rise in the path. The trail leveled out, then twisted sharply before plunging into the deep woods: the first sentry point. One sentry stood in place; as they passed, Féolan noticed the other was questioning a *Gref Orisé* prisoner. He shook his head in irritation; there had been no talk of taking prisoners and for good reason: What were they to do with this fellow now?

He caught a snatch of the prisoner's reply: "I'm sorry. I don't speak Elvish." Féolan's breath stopped in his chest. He spun around, his injured companion forgotten.

"Gabrielle?"

"GABRIELLE?" said a voice, and it was the voice she had dreamt of so often, so often that she supposed she must be dreaming yet again. It was a good dream, though, and she raised her head, focused her tired eyes and found him.

"Féolan." She took two stumbling steps toward him, and her knees buckled. He was there, swift as a cat, catching her up in his arms and holding her tight against him. Gabrielle buried her head in his shoulder and let his strength and love flow into her. They did not move or speak for a long time.

Finally she stirred. Féolan lifted her chin. Strings of hair, stiff with dirt and blood, hung before her eyes, and he tucked these back as tenderly as a mother so he could look full upon her. "Gabrielle," he said wonderingly. "How is it you are here?"

Gabrielle's face crumpled with pain. "My father is dead." The tears welled up and spilled down her cheeks. "I couldn't save him." She laid her face against his chest and sobbed.

CHAPTER 24

WHEN Gabrielle awoke she was being carried like an overgrown child through a forest tinged gray with first light. She lifted her head, disoriented, and then smiled with pleasure as a familiar voice greeted her.

"Awake at last, sleepyhead?" asked Danaïs. "A good thing. You've been putting on weight through the night, I think."

"Danaïs!"

He put her down gently, steadying her with both hands. "Hello, beautiful healer."

"Not so beautiful now," she pointed out.

"You smell very bad, as well," he agreed. "Still, it was my greatest pleasure to carry you these many miles. I had to wrestle you away from my friend Féolan. He planned to lug you along until his arms fell from their sockets." His face became serious, the brown eyes tender. "You have traveled a hard path, I think, since we last met."

"Don't make me cry again." Too late. The tears gusted through her like a storm, and Danaïs just held her while a stream of Elves passed them by. At last Gabrielle caught her breath and wiped at her eyes. Her shoulder was wet. She looked up and saw that Danaïs too had been weeping.

"I am so sorry, Gabrielle. Féolan and I both had great respect for your father. We will grieve for his family and his people."

Danaïs spoke to a nearby Elf, who nodded and headed quickly up the path. "Féolan would not let go of you until I promised to alert him if you woke," he said. "Can you walk for a while? It is a long hike still back to Stonewater."

That dawn walk through the woods might have been prescribed by a very wise healer expressly to revive Gabrielle's strong spirit. Féolan and Danaïs paced protectively on either side of her. They talked little but gave much: Safety. Love. Understanding. She walked in silence as the forest woke up around her. Birds peeped and twittered, then burst into song. The dark tree trunks became backlit in a rosy glow. The first spring leaves, that sweet pale green seen only in spring, gave the air a golden haze. As she walked, the peaceful, quiet beauty seemed to soak directly into her heart.

BY NOON THE other Elves were far ahead. The three made a little fire and ate the travel biscuits and dried apples Féolan and Danaïs had stashed in their packs. Gabrielle sat nestled against Féolan, gazing into the flames. Sometimes Féolan hummed quietly, and it seemed almost as though his voice were coming from inside her own head. The forest was drowsy and dappled under the mid-day sun, and the fire made an intimate, private circle of the three friends. The time had come to talk.

It began with a simple question: "What happened to your hair?" Gabrielle asked. Féolan's hair was still raggedly cut, though grown to about chin length.

"Oh, this is what's left of my *Gref Orisé* disguise," he began, and so unfolded the story of his journey over the mountains. Gabrielle's face clouded as he described the *Gref Orisé* way of life. That's what Derkh must return to, she thought, wondering what kind of life awaited him.

"And that's how I was nearly shot by the Verdeau army after all my adventures," he concluded. "But when I got your note I was stunned. Were you there at the pass the whole time?"

So then it was Gabrielle's turn, and when she came to Jerome's death there was more weeping, but there was comfort too, now that she was not alone.

"I was so sure I was meant to save him," she confessed, her eyes dark and lost. "So sure. I decided in my pride that I could heal him. I should have got him off the field sooner and kept him alive."

The two Elves exchanged glances. Here was a hurt that time alone would not heal.

"Gabrielle," began Féolan gently. "Surely you do not blame yourself for your father's death."

"I made a wrong judgement, Féolan," she insisted. "I would not have him crippled, so now he is dead."

"And if you had not been there, would he be alive now?"

"That's not the point," she said. "I *was* there."

"All right, then," Féolan persisted. "And how would you have taken him to safety?"

Gabrielle flinched away from his questions, a tight, defensive shrug her only answer. Féolan looked to Danaïs: help me. It was unbearable to hurt her like this. Yet to let such self-blame go unchallenged, surely that hurt was the greater?

Danaïs took up the burden. "Gabrielle, listen. There was no way to take Jerome back. He would have had to be thrown over a horse and carried at a gallop for miles until they caught up with the carts. With a broken back, how could that not kill him?

"You gave him a gift. Not the gift you wanted to give him, not life, but at least he did not die suffering and broken. He died without fear or pain, with his daughter walking beside him. That is a great mercy. You saw that hellish field. You know I speak truth."

Gabrielle was weeping again, silently, hands over her face and shoulders shaking. Féolan sat by, his own eyes red with misery. Danaïs glared at him, gestured insistently. Idiot. Go to her. Gingerly, fearing her wounded refusal, Féolan reached out and pulled her to him. She didn't refuse. She crawled into his arms, and Féolan sensed some relief in her, but she did not speak of her father again.

As THEY RESUMED their journey, Danaïs left them to run ahead. "We will have a bath and some decent food waiting for you," he promised. "And I beg you to choose the bath first."

"I'm sorry I'm so slow," Gabrielle said to Féolan. "I don't know what's wrong with me. I feel like an old lady." Instantly she regretted her words; neither of them wanted to raise that issue now.

But Féolan smoothed it over. "You're tired, Gabi. Body and soul. Anyone would be, after such an ordeal." He took her hand and laced his fingers through hers, and they walked so along the narrow trail.

The sun was slanting in from the west when Féolan announced they were nearly there. For the first time it struck Gabrielle that she was about to enter an Elvish settlement. She stopped.

"What is it?" asked Féolan. He could feel her sudden anxiety.

"Oh, Féolan, I—" She tried again. "I guess I'm shy. I'm probably the first Human to visit your home in, what? A hundred years? More? And look at me…" She laughed, without humor. "Col said I was a bloody mess, and he was exactly right."

"You won't be for long," Féolan promised.

GABRIELLE'S FIRST SIGHT of Stonewater enchanted her. The dwellings, simple well-proportioned wood structures open to the air and light, were not lined up in rows but rather placed helter-skelter, in harmony with the contours of the land. They seemed almost to have grown out of the earth. The trees had been thinned, but artfully, turning the forest into pleasant parkland. Winding pathways connected the dwellings, and she caught a glimpse of a larger structure that might be a meeting hall or royal lodge. Though she knew the settlement was well protected, she saw no guards or sentries. And yes, there was a rushing stream that leaped through the settlement from one rocky level to another, full of vigor from the mountains where it was born.

In truth, she paid close attention to her surroundings to avoid looking at the people. The Elves they passed kept a discrete silence, but Gabrielle was painfully aware of their polite curiosity.

Féolan led her to a building that was more closed in than the others, with only small windows, high near the roof. Danaïs was waiting outside the door, grinning his welcome. By his side stood a tall woman, golden-haired like him, and skipping about them like a butterfly was a beautiful girl-child, maybe eight years old. She stopped as soon as she saw Gabrielle and skittered over to her parents, staring with solemn hazel eyes.

Danaïs met her with a formal Human bow, and the foolishness of it made Gabrielle laugh in spite of her nervousness. Immediately the atmosphere lightened. "Gabrielle, meet my Lady, Celani, and my daughter, Eleara." Gabrielle's hands, at least, were clean. She made the gesture she had been taught, palm to breast and then outstretched. Celani met her hand with a welcoming smile. Eleara managed a quick smile also, then hid behind Danaïs' legs. Danaïs translated for both: "Celani bids you welcome and apologizes for not speaking your tongue. She asks if you would like to come into the bathhouse with her. Eleara, I'm afraid, is not yet completely convinced you are not a monster from her dreams."

"I can hardly blame her," said Gabrielle. She looked at Celani and said one of the two Elvish words she had learned on the trail with Féolan, "*Thank you.*" Celani opened the door, and the two women disappeared into a delicious cloud of steam.

The bathhouse was warm and clean and smelled of cedar. The sheer luxury of sinking into the waiting tub of hot water made Gabrielle's throat choke up alarmingly. Gods, you cry about everything these days, she scolded herself. She would not cry over a bath. Instead, she held her breath and slid right down under the water, soaking her grimy hair. When she emerged, Celani was waiting with soap and a soft cloth. The scent was fresh as a pine wood, and Gabrielle scrubbed every inch of herself from toes to scalp and down to the ends of her hair. Then under the water again to rinse.

As days of mud and sweat and blood sloughed off, the water darkened to rusty brown around her. She looked at it in dismay. She had wanted a second soaping and a long soak but not in this cesspool. Jumping up, she grabbed for the towel Celani had left and wrapped it around her. Celani came in with an armful of clothing and looked at Gabrielle in surprise. Then she saw the bath, and her blue eyes went round. With a quick smile, she held out her hand, as though to a child, and led Gabrielle across a little hallway to another closetlike room where—praises to the Mother—a second bath lay ready. Gabrielle slid into it with a groan of pleasure. She thought she might stay there forever.

FOR THE SECOND TIME Gabrielle was wearing someone else's clothing, but these were the lightest, softest garments she had ever touched. As she stepped through the bathhouse door, she felt like a new, damp butterfly, just emerged from its chrysalis and dressed in unfamiliar wings.

Féolan stopped mid-sentence and stared as Gabrielle appeared.

"Is something wrong?" She glanced down at her new outfit. It fit her well, she thought, though too long in the sleeve and leg. She loved the muted gray-green of the overmantle. But Féolan had the oddest look on his face. "Féolan? Does it look so ill?"

He shook his head slowly, almost dreamily, and stood and walked over to her.

"Nay, Gabrielle, forgive me. You look—" he seemed to stop himself, and his eyes lingered over her once more, from the delicate sandals to the tiny braids holding back her hair, before coming to rest on her face. "You look beautiful." But Gabrielle thought there was something forced about his smile. As their eyes met, she felt again that strange sensation of connection, as though an invisible door had opened between them. She felt what Féolan had not spoken: his bright love—and the sadness shadowing its edges.

They ate with Danaïs' family—food that was lighter and more subtle than Gabrielle was used to, and utterly satisfying. Eleara had lost her shyness and in the absence of language made friends by bringing Gabrielle little offerings: a clip for her hair, a cold fruit-berry drink, a tiny tame flying squirrel that peeked out of Eleara's pocket and accepted a nut from Gabrielle's fingers. Danaïs and Féolan translated the stream of Elvish conversation, but Gabrielle was first so hungry, and then so drowsy, that she could pay little attention. The talk flowed over her like soothing music.

It was barely dark when Féolan noticed that Gabrielle was falling asleep where she sat. He led her to a tiny guesthouse. The wide window shutters had been dropped against the chill spring night, and a small stove warmed the room. Nightwear had been laid out on the bed for her, an extra set of clothes draped over the rail and a basin of water and a comb stood ready for the morning.

A lantern, which Féolan lit, stood on a small table. At the doorway he turned, took Gabrielle in his arms and kissed her. Ignoring the warning in her brain, she wrapped her arms around his neck and kissed him back. For good or for ill, she could deny her heart no longer. A whispered good night, in Krylaise and in Elvish, and he was gone.

Sinking into the soft warmth of her bed—a real bed!—she was barely able to blow out the light before sleep claimed her.

CHAPTER 25

THE sun was high in the sky when Gabrielle stepped uncertainly out of her little cottage, wondering what to do next. She felt worlds better, almost her old self, better enough to feel curious about her new surroundings. The war against the Greffaires and its burden of death seemed far away.

Eleara waited for her outside, ready to be her guide. Slipping her small hand into Gabrielle's, she led her along the winding pathways to an open-air shelter where many Elves were gathered. It was Gabrielle's first clear sight of a group of Elves, and they were a marvel to her—so many fair, smooth faces, sparkling eyes, graceful gestures. She could think of only one Human comparison: a troupe of dancers she had seen in Blanchette, reportedly from the Tarzine lands across the Gray Sea. The women and men alike had moved with the sinewy grace of cats, heads held proudly on necks that seemed longer and straighter than any in the audience.

As they drew near, Gabrielle saw that a meal was laid out—late breakfast? Early luncheon? Whatever it was, she was famished again. Eleara led her to the buffet and waited while Gabrielle filled her plate. Today she felt more confident, her royal training returning to her, and she met the eyes of the Elves she encountered, murmuring greetings and thank-yous, smiling and shaking her head when they tried to converse further, Eleara jumping in to explain her muteness. She followed Eleara to a table where Danaïs, Celani and Féolan were just finishing their meal, aware of the surprised eyes that followed her progress.

"I guess we don't have to ask if you slept well," teased Danaïs. Féolan reached up and twined his fingers in the hair that spilled down her back, gently pulling her onto the seat beside him. Then he leaned over and kissed her cheek. Gabrielle was dismayed to feel herself blushing—like a fifteen-year-old caught smooching in a hayrick—and did her best to pretend it hadn't happened. "I must confess I can remember nothing of the night, not even dreams."

"So you call this night," mused Féolan. "Note, Danaïs, the odd ideas these Humans have."

Gabrielle grinned. So easy and pleasant it was to fall into their old bantering. "Thank-you, gentlemen, I do feel the better for it."

"You smell the better too, I must say," said Danaïs. "Doesn't she, Eleara?"

Eleara spoke to her father in Elvish, her manner serious. Danaïs sighed. "Eleara reproves me, Gabrielle. She knows I am teasing even without knowing the words and says it is unkind to make such remarks."

An Elf with a commanding manner, rather more heavyset than the rest, came over and bent down between Féolan and Danaïs, speaking quietly and rapidly. Féolan seemed both sobered and satisfied by his news. The man straightened, glanced at Gabrielle and offered his palm to her, talking a mile a minute. Gabrielle smiled and returned the gesture, while Féolan came to the rescue: "Gabrielle, this is Haldoryn. He led our raid on the Greffaire camp."

"Then I owe him my thanks, for myself and for my people. Please tell him that, Féolan."

Haldoryn looked momentarily nonplussed, but he smiled and bowed. Then clapping Féolan on the shoulder and speaking briefly once more, he strode away.

"Why do they do that?" Gabrielle demanded.

"Do what?" asked Danaïs.

"Everyone seems to assume I speak Elvish. Do they suppose that Humans, who have not even laid eyes upon them for so many years, all study their language just in case?"

She had meant it to be humorous, but Féolan gave a frustrated laugh that seemed almost angry.

"They don't realize you're Human, Gabrielle, not at first. You should look in a glass sometime. When I saw you dressed as one of us, it seemed as though ... " His voice trailed away.

Gabrielle was startled. "Are you saying I look Elvish?"

Féolan turned to Danaïs. "Am I wrong?"

Danaïs smiled at Gabrielle. "I mistook you for an Elf the first time I laid eyes on you. Of course, I was not my usual perceptive self at the time. But in those clothes, I think you will have to display your ears if you wish to be recognized as Human."

Gabrielle let her fingers glide over the remarkable softness of her new clothes. *I had never felt anything so soft as the shawl you were wrapped in.* Solange's words leaped into her head, bringing with them a thought so heady it left her weak. A foolish thought, no doubt, mere running after rainbows, yet she could not seem to thrust it away. Her very skin tingled with it.

Féolan touched her hand, reclaiming her attention. "Haldoryn had news. While we were away, the Council decided to join our forces with yours. I didn't expect it of them. Apparently the plan is to close in behind the *Gref Orisé* when they make their advance, so they will be beset from two sides."

Féolan would go, of course. He could hardly stay behind after his big speech to Council. Gabrielle stared at her plate. She thought of Tristan and Féolan on the same battlefield. Two she loved. Two more she might lose. And Tristan, she realized with a stab of regret, would be mourning his father and sister both right now, even as he prepared for battle.

"Gabrielle?" Féolan had more to tell her. "The Council of Elders wants to speak with both of us this evening."

"Me?" she squeaked. "They want to speak to me?"

"More precisely, I expect they want you to speak to them," Danaïs corrected, amused at her discomfiture.

"But why?"

"Well," said Féolan. "They want me because I know the most about the *Gref Orisé*, I expect. And you certainly know the most about the Human forces."

Gabrielle doubted she knew anything of much use about the Human forces. She remembered how Féolan had addressed the Verdeau Council, and realized how challenging that must have been. Now she was the closest thing to a foreign ambassador Verdeau had. She would do her best.

GABRIELLE AND FÉOLAN SAT on a rock ledge overlooking a waterfall, snatching a brief interlude alone. They had followed an almost invisible trail to get there, Gabrielle trying to imitate Féolan's way of gliding silently through the dense foliage. Now they sat in the sun, watching the light sparkle through the spray.

"I'm so relieved to see you looking better," confessed Féolan.

"I thought you would be several days in bed, maybe seeing our healers."

"It seems like the very air of this place makes me better," mused Gabrielle.

"And how are you liking 'this place,' anyway?" asked Féolan. "I know it is not exactly what you are used to."

"It's wonderful," said Gabrielle. "I love the way you live. Though my mind is whirling with questions."

"Name some, and I will answer if I can."

Gabrielle thought. Where to start? "Well, do you have a king or queen, or how are you governed?"

"We have no royal family," answered Féolan. "Not here in the Basin, anyway. They say there were Elf-kings and Elf-queens in Elvenhome."

"Elvenhome?"

"Where we came from, far over the ocean. No one now knows where." Féolan paused, as if seeking in his mind for that faraway land.

"So now," he said, coming out of his reverie. "Each settlement has a Council, and there is a greater Council of Elders for matters concerning all the Elves. When a councilor wishes to end his or her duty, the Council picks a successor. Or they may ask someone to serve temporarily, if their skills are needed." He laughed. "If they needed an expert on Humans, for example, they could ask me."

"Why do you laugh?"

"Oh, I have already shown myself this year too reckless by far to serve on Council. But in any case, I would be considered a little young."

"Well, and there's another question," said Gabrielle. "How old are you, anyway?"

"I will be eighty-two this summer."

"Oh." Gabrielle was deflated. "I thought you were about my age."

"I *am* about your age," he smiled. "For your information, I am just nicely into my full adulthood."

"Then how old is Danaïs?"

"Danaïs has just passed his first century. Last year, in fact."

"Does no one ever look older?" she demanded. There was something so upsetting about this. An image flashed in her mind: Solange at eighty, old and bent.

"Danaïs does not look older because he is still young," Féolan said gently. "But we do show age. It is subtle, in the eyes, mostly. Kinder than for Humans."

Gabrielle wasn't ready to face this square on. She changed the topic. "Your ears. Are there other physical differences, from Humans I mean?"

"Now that I wouldn't know," he teased. "You're the one who sees naked bodies, not me."

"Hmmm, point granted."

"Some say that in the long-ago our ears were bigger and more dramatically pointed, that they are shrinking in this new land. But then," he laughed, "they also say we were immortal."

"Immortal?" Gabrielle was shocked. "Do you believe it?"

Féolan became serious. "I look around, Gabrielle, and I see that no creature, from the greatest tree to the tiniest midge, lives forever. No, I do not believe it. Perhaps in Elvenhome we did live longer. But forever? No."

Their mood had turned somber. The war stretched its long fingers once more over Gabrielle's heart. "You have to go soon, don't you?" she said.

Féolan nodded, pulled her close. "First thing tomorrow," he said. "The delay caused by your work with Col's son brought unforeseen hope to the Basin. But time has run out. We must move quickly, or it will be too late." They sat without speaking for a long time. How strange, Gabrielle thought, that her presence at the battle had, after all, made a difference, though not in the way she had wished. She remembered how courageous she had been about the war—before she lived in its shadow. Now she knew too much. This time, she would obey her father's wishes and stay behind.

She felt Féolan take a breath before speaking. "There is one thing I would ask you before I leave." Oh, she knew what was coming, yearned for and dreaded it.

"You turned away my love once," said Féolan. "But fate has brought us together again, and I must grasp at this second chance. Gabrielle, my love for you will not waver, whatever the future holds. Will you not be my betrothed and join your life to mine?"

Gabrielle had had no time to mull over the thought that had shaken her so at the mid-day meal. She longed to share it with Féolan now, but hesitated. To raise false hopes could prove even more cruel than hard reality. It was the worst, not the best, he must be willing to face with her. She squared her shoulders and turned to him.

"Féolan, if we pledge our troth, it must be in willingness to accept the future as well as the present. It will be a bitter cup at the end." Féolan nodded, his eyes never wavering from hers. Gabrielle lifted her hand to his cheek. "I could not leave you again. If you will have me for my life's short season, then I will be yours."

CHAPTER 26

TOO soon, the urgency of war reclaimed them. Féolan was to report to his commander and prepare for battle. "I'll try to rejoin you for the evening meal," he said. "If not, Danaïs will guide you to the Council Chamber."

Alone in her little cabin, Gabrielle wondered what on earth she would do with herself in the days that stretched ahead. Danaïs, Gabrielle learned, had been assigned to the home guard because of his young child. That had surprised her. In Verdeau so many of the men in fighting prime had families that they could not have raised a viable army without them. Then again, she had seen surprisingly few children in Stonewater ... In any case, once Danaïs went on sentry duty, there would be no one—no one she knew, as yet—she could even speak to. She had just worked up the nerve to look for Celani and mime an offer of help, anything rather than wander around uselessly, when there was a knock on her door. Danaïs poked his head in.

"Are you free, Gabrielle? There is someone who would like to meet you."

Someone turned out to be Stonewater's healer, Haloan.

"He will travel with our forces tomorrow, and I expect he has his poor apprentice in a lather of preparation," explained Danaïs. "Your help will be more than welcome."

Gabrielle was relieved to find that Haloan spoke decent Kry-laise—"Quite a few of us elderly folk do," he said—and that the Healing Lodge bore many similarities to her own clinic. Haloan welcomed her graciously, complimenting her work on Danaïs' leg.

"I never had a chance to ask," said Gabrielle, turning to Danaïs. "How is your leg?"

"As you see," he said, smiling and performing an effortless deep knee-bend.

Haloan continued. "We are short one healer just now at Stonewater. Normally we are two, but my colleague traveled to another community last fall to be with her mother in her last years. My apprentice here, Towàs, can handle routine illnesses and accidents." Here the fair, strawberry-blond Elf, who had been measuring and packing herbs, offered Gabrielle a tight smile and nod. He didn't seem overly thrilled with her presence, Gabrielle thought. Haloan's next words solved that mystery. "I understand you have experience with battle injuries. It would ease my mind if you would be available to Towàs for difficult cases, or if the worst happens and our community comes under attack."

Ah, thought Gabrielle. Refugee Human swaggers in and lords it over Elvish apprentice. No wonder he's cautious. She phrased her response with care: "Please tell Towàs that I will assist him in any way I can. I will need his guidance, though, as I am unfamiliar with your medicines and methods."

"Wonderful," said Haloan. "As you know, we have much packing to do. Perhaps you could lend us a hand, and then if time permits I will show you what's where."

Danaïs ducked out and left them to it. Haloan set Gabrielle to rolling and packing bandaging. He asked her more about her experience and methods as they worked. "I met many skilled

Human healers during the last war," he remarked, "but never one who could hand-heal, or not to any significant degree." Gabrielle looked at him quizzically. "There were one or two who seemed to bolster a patient's strength or resolve, just with the force of their presence," he explained, "but none who could effect an actual repair. From what I have heard, your powers are remarkable."

There's a reason for that, Gabrielle thought; but she was not ready to speak of her birth.

"What is the most challenging wound you have healed?" Haloan asked.

Here was another thing she could not easily speak of. Her grief for Jerome was still fresh, and her sense of failure strong. Yet in Haloan's eyes she read wisdom and compassion; they spoke of long experience of loss and joy, struggle and peace. Perhaps this was what showed when Elves aged. The words came out before she had even decided, and she found she was glad to be speaking them.

"My father," she began. "He took a battle-ax to the spine." Haloan was gravely attentive, recognizing the emotional charge behind her words. He sat down across the table from her. "I wanted to reattach the nerve endings before they died back. It was very slow and difficult." She sighed and met his eyes. "I am haunted by the thought that I may have contributed to his death."

Haloan's voice was gentle. "Reconnecting nerves is complex, beyond the skill of most healers, even the most experienced. We must all learn to accept our limitations."

Gabrielle shook her head. "It's not that. Or maybe it is, in a way. I was able to make the connections." Haloan's eyes widened. "But we were on the field too long, and I was so absorbed in the healing that I never noticed..." The memory of that awful moment flashed through her, and her eyes welled with tears. "A soldier killed him, and at first I could not even tell what had happened."

Haloan did not speak or touch her, yet his very presence was a comfort. He let her recover herself and then said, "So, a soldier killed your father. Yet you feel you made an error?"

"Yes," she said. Haloan, perhaps, would understand what Danaïs and Féolan had not. "My friends point out that I had no way of taking him off the field to safety in any case, and this is true. But I did not even consider it. I was so determined to make him whole."

"Ah," said Haloan. "I think I understand. You made a sound decision, but perhaps for the wrong reason."

"Yes," said Gabrielle gratefully. "Yes, I guess that's it. I wouldn't accept a life for my father as a cripple."

"But this is a very valuable lesson," said Haloan. "Every talented healer must confront, at some time, his or her own pride and power. Your learning has not come without pain, but it comes kindly nonetheless. You could not have altered the outcome for your father, how ever you chose. So you did no harm. And in future, you will weigh choices with more care, humbled by the knowledge that the healer's desire is not always the patient's and that not one among us is perfect in judgement."

Gabrielle got up to wash her face and hands as she pondered Haloan's words. He had taken the dark, confused burden that weighed on her and given it a name. He had freed her to mourn her father's death without a choking overlay of guilt. Her awkward Elvish thank-you hardly seemed adequate.

"We can talk more about this, if you like, when I return," said Haloan. "But now we have another job to do." He set Gabrielle and Towàs to loading the bags and parcels of supplies into large panniers that would be strapped across the horses' backs.

FACING THE ELDERS of the Council once more, Féolan confirmed Haldoryn's report on their raid of the *Gref Orisé* camp, and then added that he had killed their commander. He had told Gabrielle about his encounter with Col on their way to the meeting and had been a little deflated by her subdued response.

"I thought you'd be glad," he had said.

"I am glad, for us," she said. "Only, I think of Derkh. He was good to me, Féolan, and without his father's protection I don't know how he'll fare."

Féolan's news caused a greater stir at Council. How did he think it would affect the morale of the enemy army, he was asked. He put his mind to the problem. "They are well organized," he said at last. "The structure under Col will remain intact. But his command was centralized. If there is an obvious and strong second-in-command, he will take over. But if there is a group of officers under him, I believe they will jockey for power rather than work together. There is hope, at least, that their advance has been further delayed by the need to regroup." And if not, he thought, the battle might already be lost. He had never been so aware of the fleeting march of time.

"Thank-you, Féolan." Tilumar dismissed him. "Unless there are further questions?"

As Féolan glanced around the room, his eyes rested on Councilor Orienne. He remembered her auburn hair, piercing dark eyes and keen attention from his last Elder's Council. Today, though, she seemed oblivious to the discussion at hand. She had been staring almost avidly at Gabrielle throughout Féolan's presentation.

Perhaps she disapproved of a Human presence at Council. She didn't appear hostile, though—fascinated, rather.

In any case, there were no questions, and Féolan was asked to stay and translate for Gabrielle. Tilumar welcomed her in imperfect but passable Krylaise and introduced her to the seven other Elders. Gabrielle put her hand over heart and bowed to each.

She spoke with poise, asking Féolan to begin by giving her personal thanks to the Elves of Stonewater for their hospitality. He briefly explained who she was and how she came to be there.

Gabrielle was then asked about Verdeau's numbers—how many they started with, which she knew, and how many they left with, which she didn't, though she could confirm Haldoryn's guess that the losses were not crushing. Were reinforcements expected and from where? Did they have archers, horses, other special contingents? Was the leadership of the Basin armies intact? Here she faltered a little, and Féolan, wanting to spare her reliving Jerome's death, asked if she wished him to tell the story. She shook her head, squared her shoulders and lifted her chin in the gesture of determination already familiar to him.

"King Jerome, my father," she began, "was killed on the field." She took a breath to steady herself. "But General Fortin, his military commander, directs our forces, and my brother Tristan will support him. The Verdeau army will not falter."

"May I ask a question?" It was Orienne. "I understand you were captured on the battlefield by the *Gref Orisé*. I have been long away from Humans, but I did not think it was usual for their women to fight. How is it that you happened there?"

"I am a bo—a healer," Gabrielle amended, using the Elvish term. "I was treating the wounded, not fighting. I went onto the field when my father was injured."

Orienne gazed at Gabrielle long and intently. Féolan could feel Gabrielle fighting to be still under her gaze. At last Orienne dropped her eyes and said in heavily accented Krylaise, "I am sorry. That was uncourteous." Switching back to her fluid Elvish, she added, "May I speak privately to you after? I would explain my ill manners."

CHAPTER 27

FÉOLAN waited with Gabrielle in the drafty entranceway for over an hour, Gabrielle becoming more and more jittery beside him. "I don't know what she wants or why she looked at you so," he said patiently, yet again. "We'll just have to—" The door opened, and Orienne slipped out.

"They can finish up without me," she said. "Is there somewhere quiet we can go?"

They went to Féolan's dwelling. Small but spacious, beautifully crafted though sparely furnished, it would be filled with light and birdsong when the windows were opened. Now they were shuttered against the cool spring night, and the effect was snug and private. He lit a fire and several ceramic wall lamps, poured three goblets of wine and sat down to translate. Though there were chairs and a table at the far end of the room, they sat instead on deep curved cushions, covered in shades of green, gray and blue, pulled close around the fire. Gabrielle watched how Orienne tucked her feet neatly behind her, looking elegantly at ease rather than sprawled, and tried to arrange herself the same way.

"I hope you will forgive me for staring so and at a guest," Orienne began. "It is not my custom. But when you walked in the Council Chamber, I thought for one moment that you were my niece, whom I have not seen in nearly thirty years. You look so like her, I cannot tear my eyes away."

Féolan nodded, ready to smile at the chance likeness, thank Orienne for her time and bid her goodnight.

But Gabrielle spoke up. "What happened to her?" she asked. This was not just polite small talk: her voice trembled with tension. Féolan had never seen Gabrielle so nervous.

"She and her husband shared a love of wandering," Orienne replied. "She wished to see the ocean and her husband's homeland in south Barilles. They set off on a journey to the coast."

South Barilles? thought Féolan, curious now. As far as he knew, the Elves had long ago left the coast to Human settlement.

"I wondered if Wyndra was wise to go, for she had a newborn baby. But she laughed and said, 'Easier now than when she's walking!' She was ever headstrong and fearless... even with her heart."

Féolan looked up sharply at the hint of bitterness in Orienne's voice, wondering if he had read this story aright. Orienne nodded. "He was Human, a scholar who came to Fernrill settlement to study our histories."

Waves of emotion poured off Gabrielle as he translated—startling, churning, mixed-up blasts of feeling that Féolan could not begin to interpret. Gabrielle was shivering so violently Féolan was afraid she was ill. He put his arm around her, but she didn't seem to notice him at all. Her eyes never left Orienne as the sad tale continued.

"Neither of them ever returned. After six months had passed, we sent people searching for them. We never found them. It will be twenty-eight years this autumn since she left."

"My parents found me that year, hidden in a hollow log by the sea amongst a group of murdered adults," Gabrielle blurted out.

It took Féolan a minute to grasp the meaning of her words. His body seemed to comprehend before his mind: it felt electric with excitement. His heart skipped and throbbed in his chest like a skin drum. He gave the rhythm words: Let it be true. Let it be true.

Gabrielle gave him an urgent look, waiting for his translation, then softened at his expression. "My mother told me only this winter," she said. "But Féolan, it might have meant nothing."

"What does she say?" Orienne now, trying to understand, with her rusty Krylaise, the high emotion in the room. Féolan tried to clear his head and repeat Gabrielle's words. Slowly Orienne reached out her slim hands and clasped Gabrielle's between them. They were lost in each other. "My sister's daughter is dead, then," she said slowly. "And my great-niece is alive. Gabrielle, I believe I first laid eyes on you at your naming ceremony. You were just one week old, and your mother named you Twylar."

"I need to be sure," Gabrielle whispered. She reached with shaky fingers for a rough rawhide cord around her neck. It was long, tucked deeply down her front. She tugged at it. "I didn't want it to look worth stealing," she explained. "So I put it on this leather. But … " Now, at last, Féolan saw the glitter of silver at the end of the cord. He leaned forward, anxious to see. It took one glance to identify the tiny necklace: a babystone. He had watched Danaïs fasten just such a one around Eleara's neck on her name day. Orienne was weeping now, cradling the little jewel in her hand as though a baby still wore it.

Gabrielle, distressed, turned to Féolan. "We give such a stone to babies on their nameday," he explained. Stars above, all he wanted to do was take this woman in his arms, but this was her story, not his, and she did not want him now. Not yet. "The stone—"

"The stone is called *jeldeñi*," said Orienne. "It is the stone of your mother's house. We all admired how your babystone matched your eyes. They were lighter, then."

Gabrielle burst into tears, and now Féolan's arms were welcome. He wrapped her tight, remembering Gabrielle's sudden tension over their mid-day meal and her hesitation at the falls, imagining how the pieces of her life must have fallen into place with nothing but speculation to hold them together. If she'd shown me the damn necklace I could have told her, he thought. But that wasn't quite true, was it? He could have told her enough to change the odds, but now it was for sure, and her life was forever changed.

BUT HOW WAS it changed? Gabrielle did not know how to find the words, or the courage, for all the questions that clamored in her heart. She watched Orienne refill the tall wine flutes, finding a soothing familiarity in the gesture. No stopping now. She had to know.

"Orienne, what does it mean—to be ... what I am?"

"To be half-Elven? I'm afraid it is not always an easy life." Orienne spoke to both of them, now that she saw how it was with them. But her eyes lingered on Gabrielle.

"Your mother asked me to study this question before your birth. I visited many settlements in search of an answer. Most of our knowledge dates from the last war against *Gref Oris*. That was a long and bitter struggle with great losses on both sides, and in such times Elves and Humans alike are more reckless with their love. Who can blame them for grasping at what happiness they can, when death looms so likely? But not all died, and an unusual number of half-Elven babies were born the next year."

Orienne sipped at the amber wine and gazed into the fire, gathering her thoughts. She sighed. "There is no pattern, it seems, to how the Elvish and Human traits will blend in any one person. Some of the children seemed almost entirely Human, with only subtle signs—unusually keen eyesight, perhaps, or nimble, clever fingers—of their Elvish side. Some were very Elf-like, in looks and even abilities." Her eyes returned to Gabrielle. "Your mother was a skilled healer, strong in the gift of the hands. This, I understand, she has passed on to you."

Gabrielle felt a rush of wonder. For the first time her connection with the woman who bore her seemed real. It was as though Wyndra had reached down through time and handed Gabrielle a torch: a gift and a responsibility.

Orienne had spoken again and stopped, while Gabrielle was wrapped in these thoughts. Féolan touched her hand and translated: "Those with a more even mix of traits often had a more difficult time. Never really at home with either race, they wandered as minstrels or traders. There were a few scholars and teachers among them and outlaws too."

Gabrielle only half-heard this report. She already knew where her path lay. Yet she could not bring herself to voice the question on which so much hinged.

Féolan's arm tightened around her, and she leaned into his steady strength. His voice was the merest murmur in her ear: "We have already pledged to find joy in what we have and not despair at what might have been. Nothing we learn now will change that."

"I know what you would ask." Orienne leaned toward Gabrielle, reached for her hand and held it between her own. Gabrielle searched the older woman's face—how strange, that her age had somehow become clear as they spoke—and saw the sadness before she heard the words. Poor Féolan, she thought. Despite his brave words, she knew what he had hoped for.

"I wish," said Orienne, "that I could promise you a long life among us, Gabrielle, but I'm afraid that life span is as uncertain as the other half-Elven traits. I know of one, born soon after the war, who lives yet, though age weighs heavily upon him."

Had she misunderstood that? One look at Féolan removed all doubt—he fairly hummed with suppressed excitement. But Orienne cut in hastily: "Please, do not let that mislead you. It is an unusual case. And at the other end, there were some whose lives were much shorter."

"How much shorter?" Gabrielle was deliberately blunt. It was time to put her fear to rest, whatever the answer.

Orienne's eyes grew sorrowful, her voice gentle. "A few lived barely two hundred years. I'm afraid you cannot count on more than that. I am sorry."

Gabrielle blinked. Her life had just been more than doubled, and Orienne was sorry! A breathless laugh escaped her. Her eyes met Féolan's—was she crazy to be so happy? And he was smiling at her, that smile that melted all the bones in her body.

"Two hundred years, Féolan," she whispered. "We have—"

She never got to finish. Féolan had pulled her into his arms, and his kiss drove the words right out of her head.

Not that she cared.

MORE WINE AND MORE TALK, and at last Orienne stood and kissed Gabrielle on the forehead and said, "We will celebrate your return in true Elvish style, Gabrielle. But the celebration must wait, I'm afraid, until we are done with these *Gref Orisé* invaders. In the meantime, may I be the one to welcome you into your family? It is a great joy to me that you live and that we have found each other."

It was late. Féolan walked her to the little guesthouse, and Gabrielle was grateful that he did not press her to speak as they threaded their way through the still night. She knew his thoughts brimmed with the life they could now plan together. Hers were a more complicated mixture of joy and sorrow, not ready to be spoken. The stars looked far away and cold this late at night. Did their silvery patterns foretell a person's path in life, as some claimed? She felt strangely alone for one who has had just reclaimed her family.

At Gabrielle's doorstep, Féolan brushed his knuckles along her cheek. "Are you all right?" he asked.

Gabrielle nodded. "It's a lot to get used to."

And then it was time for their goodbyes, for Féolan would be gone before first light. Gabrielle drew her hand slowly from his elbow to his fingertips, memorizing the swell of muscle in the forearm, the smooth skin, the intricate join of bones and tendon at the wrist, the long fingers. She tried not to hear the voice that added, *in case he does not return.* Some time passed before she looked up.

"All the words and phrases that people use on occasions such as this—take care, stay safe, come back soon—stick in my throat like a burr and refuse to come out," she confessed. "I can think of nothing to say that feels true in my heart except that I love you."

"It is all I need to hear," said Féolan.

THAT NIGHT IN BED, the bits and pieces of Gabrielle's life wheeled around her, assembling and coming apart in random combinations. *You are my real mother,* she had told Solange, and it was true. Her father had died in her arms on a battlefield.

That too was true. How did that fit with Wyndra, the Elf who had borne and lost her so long ago, or the mysterious man who had won her love?

How were Gabrielle DesChênes of Verdeau and Twylar of Fernrill to become one person?

And through the long night the other question, the fear that gnawed at the edges of her heart though she refused to give it words, shadowed her dreams: What if Féolan should not return?

CHAPTER 28

GABRIELLE woke in the thin darkness before dawn. She sat, hugging her knees, the day yawning empty and anxious before her. Already it was obvious she was not going to be much good at waiting.

But the day was not as difficult as she had feared. Celani and Eleara came by in the early morning, and from Eleara's spirited charades and the bundled clothing they both carried Gabrielle understood it was laundry day. She gathered up her own soiled clothes and followed them first to the bathhouse, where Celani showed her how to draw and set water to heating, and then to a place about a half-mile from the settlement where the stream quieted into a deep pool, edged with flat rocks. Here they soaped and rinsed their clothes in water so icy their hands went numb. If my father could see me now, scrubbing away like a washerwoman, thought Gabrielle, surprising herself with a thought untainted by the troubled grief of days past. She had not laid eyes on a servant since her arrival at Stonewater, though someone must cook the meals that appeared under the large pavilion.

Eleara lay flat on her stomach, watching for crayfish and trout, hissing with the cold as she plunged her arm in to the shoulder after a frog. By the time the clothes were hung out, the baths were ready. Eleara's idea of a good wash included much splashing, spouting and laughter. And though Celani seemed to be apologizing for her playfulness, it was just what Gabrielle needed. She left their company having learned the words for "cold," "frog," "bath" and "stop it," at least she thought that's what they meant, and feeling better about her ability to get along without a translator.

She didn't need to, though. In the afternoon she made her way to the Healing Lodge, nervous but determined to make some kind of overture with Towàs. He greeted her pleasantly, having apparently decided she wasn't much threat after all, but without language it was difficult to make headway. She was leafing through the books of healing lore he had shown her—she couldn't, of course, read the words, but there were illustrations of herbs and treatments—when an Elvish woman, dark-haired and about five months' pregnant, entered the Lodge. She greeted Gabrielle in fluent Krylaise: "I am Nehele. I am one of Féolan's scouts." She patted her swelling belly and smiled. "Off duty, for obvious reasons. I would be happy to act as your interpreter in the days to come."

Nehele and Gabrielle liked each other on sight, and the afternoon passed quickly. Towàs was happy to share his knowledge of medicinal herbs and their uses, and Gabrielle found that with Nehele she was not shy to try out Elvish words and phrases. As night fell, Nehele invited Gabrielle to dine with her. "It is Danaïs' last night with his family," she said, "and my first night alone. I would be glad of the company."

The two women talked late into the night, and Gabrielle realized how much she had missed the company and confidences of women. Nehele recounted her first scouting ventures into Human settlements and asked about the customs and sights that had puzzled her. Gabrielle had plenty of questions in return. Before they were done Gabrielle had told, for the first time, how she had met Féolan and the story of her birth. Nehele shook her head, her dark eyes bright with wonder. "Someone must make a song about this," she declared. "It is like a tale from long ago."

First let him return alive, Gabrielle thought. As if by mutual consent, neither had raised the specter of war that evening.

"I'll walk a ways with you toward your dwelling," Nehele insisted, as Gabrielle made to leave. The night was soft and misty, smelling of spring, and Gabrielle thought again how far away the Greffaire invasion seemed in this sheltered place.

"Have you attended a birth before?" Nehele asked Gabrielle as they paced along the dark pathway.

"Yes, many times," smiled Gabrielle. "I love catching babies."

"Perhaps," offered Nehele, "if you are here, you will be with me when my baby comes. I know Haloan can do it, but there's something about having another woman that's more comfortable, don't you think?"

"Many women feel that way," agreed Gabrielle. Still, she was deeply honored that Nehele would entrust such a thing to her on such short acquaintance. She began to feel that perhaps Stone-water could, in time, become her home.

TRISTAN NARROWED HIS EYES and scanned the horizon again, searching for the dark smudge of dust cloud or glint of reflected light that would announce the Greffaire offensive. Gods, he needed them to come before he went crazy with waiting. Why the Greffaires had not followed on the retreating Verdeau troops' heels was anyone's guess. Three days it had been now since that disastrous battle—time to rendezvous with the Maronnais rein-forcements, choose the most favorable site to deploy the men and fine-tune their defense strategy. That extra time had been a godsend, but now the Basin defense force was as great as it would ever be, and Tristan lusted for revenge.

He was much changed in spirit. The trademark grin had not brightened his face since they had tallied their losses the day after the retreat, and his eyes were flat and hard. Jerome's death had been a blow. No one could say why the king had been so deep in the field, or why he had remained after the horns had blown. The seeming carelessness of it rankled, but Jerome had come as a warrior, and a warrior expects to risk his life. It was the loss of Gabrielle that nearly undid him. Through the long, uneasy nights, Tristan wrestled with questions that had no answers: How had she missed the retreat? Why had he not watched over her more carefully, protected her more closely? How would he explain her death to Solange? She should have been safely away with the other bonemenders. That his sister, extraordinary as she was, could be killed through some random accident or stroke of ill luck ate at his natural optimism like a cancer.

Just that afternoon, Fortin himself had lectured Tristan about the importance of control in battle and the dangers of rage. Tristan knew his men studied him uneasily when they thought he took no notice. But he was not looking for his own death in the coming battle. He was looking for an accounting.

Tristan remained on the ridge long after the relief sentries arrived. He watched the sky deepen to indigo, watched the moon rise and spill its light down the road that lay like a river heading north. When the stars had defined themselves into cold white brilliance, Tristan headed back to camp. He would eat and rest, but he would take no pleasure in it.

THE CLATTER OF HOOFBEATS caught their attention before the door of the Healing Lodge was thrown open. One look at the travel-worn Elf who stood panting before them was enough to make Gabrielle's stomach clench: an envoy, and the word he brought was not good.

He strode over to Towàs, who looked almost comically startled, and thrust a roll of parchment into his hand. Then he sprawled in a chair to catch his breath. Gabrielle fetched the envoy a drink of water, and then another, while Towàs read the note. His expression was first bewildered, then panicky. When the parchment drifted unnoticed from his hand, Nahele took it up. Scanning quickly, she translated for Gabrielle.

"It says Haloan has taken ill with a high fever. They have brought him to Silverdeep, the nearest settlement. They ask that Towàs come now to replace him as the *Gref Orisé* army is already south of them and they expect to engage within the day."

The two women looked at Towàs. He was trying to rise to the occasion, but it was clear he felt ill-prepared for the summons. His voice was strained as he spoke to the messenger. Nahele murmured a translation in Gabrielle's ear: "He says of course he will come, but that he has rarely even set a broken bone by himself. That he is still but an apprentice." Towàs turned now to the two women, eyes almost pleading. "He is afraid of causing harm through lack of experience," explained Nahele. "He asks your counsel."

Gabrielle looked at the young apprentice and saw herself at seventeen. However willing, he could not fill the place of a seasoned healer. Her path was clear. "Tell Towàs I will go," she said quietly. "I cannot treat the people here properly. I do not know them or these medicines well enough. But I do have battle experience. It only makes sense that he should stay and I should go."

In less than an hour, she was mounted on Arda, ready to ride with the envoy. Thank the stars there was a horse here who would take a bridle, she thought, as she settled herself on nothing but a blanket. Towàs strapped a pack of extra supplies across Arda's back. He touched palms with her, his eyes troubled.

"Nahele," said Gabrielle, her gaze still on the apprentice. "Tell Towàs he must have no shame in this. It is as Haloan taught me: A healer has to think first what is best for the patients. It takes courage to do that." Towàs nodded, offered a reluctant smile. Gabrielle leaned down from Arda to embrace Nahele. "Will you tell Celani and Eleara that I've gone?"

The messenger urged her on, and they left the little settlement at a canter. Gabrielle was surprised to find she was glad to be going. With no saddle, she just hoped she could keep her seat long enough to get there.

FÉOLAN HAD BEEN dogging the *Gref Orisé* army since late morning. He had been placed at the head of the chain of advance scouts in the hope that he might overhear something of value. However, he had only been able to get within earshot a few times. Since the Elvish raid, the *Gref Orisé* had become more cautious travelers, and mounted spotters now eyed the forested margins of the road.

The Elves would have been gratified to learn just how jumpy those spotters were. The *Gref Orisé* soldiers had been badly shaken to find that their powerful army, and even their feared commander, could be so vulnerable. Worse, somehow, was the fact that they had no inkling who their attackers were. One disoriented, rattled soldier had ventured the opinion that they were beset by the vengeful ghosts of their dead foes, and the notion had spread and taken root among the normally tough-minded *Gref Orisé*. Many in the army found the narrow road and thick woodlands of the Maronnais highlands brooding and oppressive and marched with hidden unease.

Féolan, trailing behind the long column of men, did not at first take the meaning of the sudden shouting and jostling ahead. Only when the unit heads started hustling their men into position and soldiers went scrambling for their armor did he realize that they had made contact with the Basin forces. Silently he worked his way back to the closest scout to pass on the news. It was time.

CHAPTER 29

TRISTAN stood up in his stirrups to catch his bearings. Two hours into the battle, he still could not judge who had the advantage. With the Verdeau and the Maronnais troops combined, the Greffaires were only marginally greater in force. It would not be a quick victory, either way.

There. He had been searching for a way through the sea of frightened conscripts in order to engage with the real soldiers who would decide this battle. Tristan shouted to his men and pointed. They formed up and charged, mowing a path through the conscripts toward the first wedge of armored men. Closing in, they abandoned their horses. They had found in the last engagement that fighting full-armored soldiers on horseback was not much use, except for those few who could use a bow effectively while riding. Mostly, it got the horses killed. Tristan's men worked in teams of three, as they had practiced: two to single out and strip a warrior, one to watch their backs. Fortin would be proud of me, Tristan thought with grim amusement. He fought carefully, with cold determination. He cared about his men too much to give way to the recklessness that goaded him.

They fought thus for an hour, making slow but definite headway, until Tristan found himself drawn against a sword blade as like unto his own as a twin. He checked his lunge and looked to his foe—and the eyes that stared back at him peered from a helmet bearing the green stripe of Verdeau, a helmet whose familiar crest pulled the breath from his body in a hiss of rage. With narrow, dangerous eyes Tristan examined the man who had picked over the King of Verdeau's carcass like a carrion crow: Jerome's sword in his hand, Jerome's helm on his head—and jingling on a string of silver and gold trinkets slung over the heavy armor, the copper earring his father had worn for as long as Tristan could remember.

With a howl of fury he fell upon the Greffaire. Tristan's sword plunged under the collar of the helm and up, and the man fell back, spouting blood. In the red haze that descended over him there was no thought of self-control or strategy. There was only his sword, the lust to drive it deep into the enemy and the wrath that fed his strength.

Tristan plunged into the Greffaire ranks like a madman, and none could withstand him. His sword rose and fell, cutting a swath through living men as though through a field of grain. His own men struggled to stay with him, both alarmed and stirred by the wild offensive.

WHEN HIS HEAD finally cleared, it took Tristan only a moment to see that he had engineered his own death. He and the little band fighting their way through to him were deep into the Greffaire lines—and they were all alone. For himself he was content to have cost the enemy dear, but he reviled himself for playing so free with the lives of the men who followed his lead. "Go back!" he yelled to them as the sea of Greffaire soldiers closed in around him. "Get back to your lines!" He set his sword and prepared to die.

The first soldier who came at him had more bravado than skill. Tristan easily sidestepped his headlong rush and sliced across the exposed back of the knee as the momentum carried the man past. The Greffaire crashed to the ground, the tendons severed.

But four leaped in to take his place, and Tristan was hard beset just to keep his feet and parry their strikes. All that was left to him was this grim and hopeless defense, until the inevitable error—or simple exhaustion—claimed him. Already his breath came in labored gasps, and his strength began to waver under the rain of blows.

The heavy arc of an ax swung in from his left. He caught it with his shield, but the angle was too extreme to meet it properly. Tristan's arm crumpled with the impact; the rim of the shield slammed into his shoulder, knocking him sideways. Through waves of pain he fought to keep his footing, nearly regained it—then a powerful downward slice forced him to one knee as he threw up his arm to deflect it.

The end was a matter of seconds now, no more. Tristan's enemies paused, momentarily, as if savoring their victory as they raised their weapons for the kill.

Damned if I will die a faceless death, Tristan thought. Let them look on the man they kill! He swept off his helmet, raised his sword defiantly, sucked in a final burning breath. "For Verdeau!" he yelled. They seemed as good last words as any.

THE ELVES HAD WAITED until the commotion of battle was a terrible clamor in the sky to come out of cover and rank up. There would be no hiding in the forest this time, but they could at least come upon the enemy unawares. Without battle cry or drums, horns or heralds, they appeared, a stern and silent host behind an army that took no notice of their presence.

Four volleys of arrows, loosed in quick succession, found their marks before the *Gref Orisé* realized their source. Several more stopped the first disordered counterattacks. By the time a commander was found to organize a concerted front against the Elves, *Gref Orisé* soldiers lay thick on the ground before them.

Now it was close fighting against these men clad in metal, and Féolan remembered vividly the claustrophobic misery of those casings. To die trapped within them was as ugly a death as he could imagine, and he felt no disadvantage from his own exposed flesh. Neatly, almost surgically, he stepped in and slashed at the leather shoulder strap of the heavy soldier before him. Blocking the man's powerful return stroke, he kicked out hard at the knee joint. His opponent staggered, flailed momentarily but did not fall as Féolan had hoped. His comrade, Islain, fighting on his right side, seized the opportunity and swung his blade in a ringing broadside to the head. Even through the helmet it brought the man down—and soon after he was dead.

Féolan and his unit fought on, slowly making inroads into the enemy's rear flank. He could summon no hatred for the men he killed, only bitter anger at the tyrant who had sent them here and the conviction that they must be stopped.

Shouting, just a little ahead, caught his ear. He thought it was a Basin accent, though in the uproar it was hard to be sure. The scene before him unfolded in brief glimpses, snatched in the heartbeat pauses between thrust and block, feint and strike: a line of *Gref Orisé* soldiers, moving away from him; a lone Verdeau soldier, green stripe on his helm; the *Gref Orisé* on the attack, wolves after their prey.

Féolan had his opening, thrust at an exposed underarm and shoved his opponent to the side. Now he was directly behind the line of soldiers. The Verdeau man had fallen to his knees, was just visible through a gap in the ring surrounding him. Feolan watched as the soldier suddenly reached up, ripped off his helmet and with a hoarse cry yelled, "For Verdeau!" The soldier's thick blond hair fell free, his blue eyes blazed defiance. The *Gref Orisé* lifted their swords high.

"Tristan!" cried Féolan and leaped at the nearest soldier, clubbing him to the ground. Islain was with him, the others close behind. A sword fell; Tristan parried. Two of the attacking *Gref Orisé* whirled away from Tristan to face this new threat. Soon Féolan stood back-to-back with Tristan, his head still ringing with alarm and relief.

"Well met, my friend!" he shouted. He could see, now, Tristan's men, only a few strides away, working steadily toward them. His own Stonewater Elves closed in, so that it was the *Gref Orisé* who now began to feel trapped.

"Féolan! Never have I been so glad to see an unexpected friend," returned Tristan. He took advantage of the sudden press of allies to catch his breath, and as his chest heaved for air his face darkened. Here, he thought, is another who will mourn my sister and must be told.

"Tristan," called Féolan over his shoulder, "your sister Gabrielle sends her love and says you should be more careful!"

For one terrible moment, Féolan feared the shock of his words would be the death of his newly rescued friend. Tristan dropped his arms, turned and gaped at Féolan.

"She's alive? Is she safe? Where?"

"Watch yourself!" Féolan roared. Tristan scrambled back into his defensive posture. However, it was not skill at arms but the beatific smile with which he greeted the attacking Greffaire soldier that saved him. In the midst of such wreckage, Tristan's grin of relief completely unnerved the fellow, who checked his ax swing and ran off in search of a less maniacal foe.

There was little chance for talk through the rest of that bloody afternoon. Tristan and Féolan fought side by side, as did their men, and though the work of war was as fearsome and terrible as before, each was bolstered by the other's presence.

When the tide finally turned in their favor, it gathered momentum quickly. By nightfall the invasion was over. The few hundred *Gref Orisé* who had broken through the thin ranks of Elves ran desperately for home. The conscripts who had had the sense to bolt early from the battlefield were not pursued. Few others were left alive.

CHAPTER 30

IN a protected hollow a few hundred yards behind the battle-field, a select group of men met in King Drolet's tent. Present were the king himself and his First General, Roche, for La Maronne; Prince Tristan and First General Fortin for Verdeau; First General Moreau for Gamier; and for the Elves, Jalanil of the Elders' Council, Haldoryn as chief military officer, and Féolan, first ambassador of Stonewater and translator.

The gathering was brief, involving as it did only two items of business: introductions and mutual expressions of friendship and gratitude, and organizing the wretched aftermath of battle. The wounded must be found, treated and brought home. The dead, thousands of them, must be disposed of. King Drolet offered accommodation in Gaudette for anyone requiring it. More extensive discussions would wait.

Féolan and Tristan sat down for the discussions. They had both seen heavy fighting from the first moments of battle and neither was inclined to stand on ceremony. Tristan's left arm was tied up in a makeshift sling Féolan had made by ripping a foot of fabric from the bottom of his tunic. It was broken just above the wrist, and Féolan could tell by the way Tristan shifted restlessly in his seat that the pain of it was beginning to tell. As for himself, he suspected there were broken bones in his right hand, but he had escaped major injury. Even so, there seemed to be no place on his body that did not hurt. Few of today's warriors would have a comfortable night's sleep.

As soon as they were dismissed, Féolan went to Tristan. "Let's get you to a healer and have that arm set," he said.

Tristan shook his head. "Afraid not. Not yet, anyway. They have their hands full right now with worse injuries than mine."

Féolan didn't like the white, strained look around Tristan's lips and eyes. As royalty, Tristan could undoubtedly demand—and get—preferential treatment. But his judgement was sound. Another man's life could hang in the delay caused by plastering a simple break. Féolan wouldn't want that on his head, either.

"Why don't we see how busy our Elvish healers are?" he asked. "There are fewer of us to mend, after all."

The two men skirted the edge of the battlefield and walked up the road to the Elvish healing lodge. Féolan was limping now, only just realizing how badly he had wrenched his knee. Propping themselves against the trunk of a huge old cedar a stone's throw away from the tents, they tried to take stock of the scene before them. The line of waiting patients was shorter than at the Human clinic tents, but it was impossible to tell how critical their injuries were. Everyone, including Tristan and Féolan, was so blood-spattered and streaked that all looked, from a distance, on the verge of death.

"Can we sit while we wait?" suggested Tristan. "I pretty much have to, actually." He eased down to the ground with a grimace. "Right. Now tell me about Gabi. Where did you see her, and how is she?"

Féolan didn't answer right away. He was staring at the chestnut-brown braid hanging down one healer's back. The square of her shoulders, their rise and fall as she wrapped bandaging around and around a patient's bare chest, was familiar. So was the way she stretched out her back and neck when she was done.

"I think," he said, "that you can ask her yourself. Look there."

GABRIELLE TOOK A LAST appraising look at her bandaging. She tucked in a stray end and nodded approval. Helping her patient to his feet, she guided him over to the row of pallets behind the Healing Lodge, where he could rest and recover. She signaled to the healer overseeing the recovery area, who would dole out medicines and watch for fever or other complications.

What a strange experience it was working with healers who shared her methods but not her language. Not that there had been time for talk. Up until this last hour she might have been in a recurring nightmare back at the Skyway Pass. One emergency after another. One hacked and bloody body after another. Elvish or Human, the suffering was the same.

But there had been fewer. Now, at last, they were down to the less critical cases, at least until more survivors were brought in from the field. She cast her eyes along the row of waiting casualties, and then something made her look up.

Two men, dark hair and fair, both as sorry-looking as she had ever seen them. Both alive.

Gabrielle flew out of the tent and over to the great tree where they were propped like rag dolls. Dropping to her knees, she opened her arms and gathered them in—but tenderly, for her healer's eyes had noted Tristan's sling.

EVEN HIS OWN SISTER couldn't tend to him right away; Tristan had to settle for a cup of evil-tasting herbal tea, which he admitted after ten minutes or so did ease his pain. I should have asked for some too, Féolan thought ruefully; his hand and knee sang out now in time to his pulse. He passed the hour's wait telling Tristan how he had unwittingly rescued Gabrielle from the *Gref Orisé*.

"She went after my father, didn't she?" asked Tristan.

"Yes. But I think that is a tale for her to tell."

Gabrielle had just come for Tristan when a runner approached Féolan.

"My lord Féolan, they wish to question a *Gref Orisé* prisoner. If you are able, will you come and speak to him?"

"You will have to help me walk, I'm afraid," replied Féolan. "But yes, lead me on."

He had expected a bound soldier. Instead the messenger led him to a crude haycart tucked away at the far edge of the field. A couple of Stonewater Elves stood peering in. They turned to Féolan, their expressions doubtful. "We do not know what to do with this one."

Féolan looked inside with trepidation. Glaring back at him was a scrawny boy in mid-adolescence at most. Face pale and clammy under chopped dirty hair. Fear palpable under the bravado. And sick. There was no question he was seriously ill.

Gabrielle's fears had come true. With the shock of Col's death and the momentum of the invasion, Féolan doubted anyone had treated Derkh at all. It looked as though he had been tossed in the cart as an afterthought.

Féolan looked at the boy, his gaze steady and kind. Slowly, the young man's frightened hostility faded.

Then, very quietly, so only the two of them could hear, Féolan said, "I am a friend of Gabrielle's. Are you Derkh?"

The emotions chasing one another across the boy's face would have been comical if he had not been in such desperate shape:

Shock. Relief. Hope. Worry. His first words were touching in their selflessness: "Is she all right?"

Féolan smiled. "She's fine. And she'll want to see you right away, I expect. She won't be at all happy at the state you're in."

Derkh eyed the tall Elves around his cart. "Aren't they going to kill me?"

"We aren't in the habit of killing sick boys," said Féolan briskly. "They are going to pull this cart to our Healing Lodge, where Gabrielle will try to put right whatever has gone wrong with your wound."

"Infected," the boy grunted. He lay back on the straw and closed his eyes. "She warned me."

GABRIELLE WAS PLASTERING Tristan's arm as Féolan approached them.

"Ho, there's a fair-weather friend," declared Tristan. "You managed to disappear for the screaming and yelling part, I see. Where were you when I needed an arm to grip?"

Gabrielle knew Tristan was exaggerating but not inventing "the screaming and yelling" part. Bonesetting could be a rough job, and after several hours of jostling, his arm had been swollen and tender. It bothered her still that she could not take the time to speed the healing and soothe the hurts, not just for Tristan but for all the injured she had treated this day.

"Hold still, Tris," murmured Gabrielle. "Give it a chance to harden." She rinsed the plaster off her hands and took a critical look at Féolan. He favored his right hand, she saw, on top of the limp. "Right, you're next. Let's have a look at that leg."

"There's someone here who needs you more, Gabrielle," said Féolan, pointing to the cart parked just outside the tent. Drying her hands on the back of her skirt, Gabrielle walked over and looked over the wooden side.

"Ah, dark gods," she whispered. "Look at you." She reached down to feel Derkh's forehead, though she didn't have to. Heat almost shimmered off his body. Remorse stabbed at her. "I shouldn't have left you."

"Of course you should have," Derkh snapped. He seemed older than Gabrielle remembered. "This way we both get to live." Then his manner softened, became childlike. "Can you save me again, Gabrielle?"

Her throat was tight as she thought of what her young friend had been through. "I'll do my very best, Derkh. I promise."

THE NIGHT CRAWLED by as Gabrielle fought for Derkh's life. The skin around his wound was shiny with swelling, a hot angry red that streaked off along the path of the surrounding blood vessels. She was angry too at the callousness of the men who had left him thus, but she had to let it go. There was no place for such thoughts in the healing trance.

By morning the fever was lower, and the red streaks were gone. The infection was localized in a tight circle around the wound itself, and Gabrielle dared to leave him long enough to go in search of breakfast. She found travel biscuits and tea and sat under the big cedar tree to eat and rest. Soon, she thought, she would have to see if she was needed on any cases more critical than Derkh's. The Human bonemenders would doubtless be glad of her help as well, when she could manage it. The very thought was exhausting. Her eyes closed against the morning sun.

When she started awake, Tristan and Féolan were back, loung-
ing on either side of her. Neither looked much better for their
night's "sleep."

"Hi. Rough night?" she asked.

"We could ask you the same," noted Tristan.

"How's the young lad?" asked Féolan.

"Some better," she said. "I need to get back to him soon." She
dippered out medicinal tea for both of them, and bullied them
into drinking it, and checked over Tristan, proclaiming him as
well as could be expected. Then she took Féolan by the good
hand, led him to the Lodge and sat him down. The knee, she
concluded, would heal itself, but she wrapped it up to give him a
little support in the meantime. Then she laid the hurt hand in hers
and just held it, remembering the night they had said farewell.
His good hand reached up and stroked the side of her face, and
without even thinking she bent down and kissed him.

Tristan was grinning at them broadly. "Looks like you two
are on good terms again!" Guiltily, Gabrielle realized how much
Tristan still didn't know. She smiled weakly.

"I guess that's one way of putting it. I have a lot to tell you Tris,
when there's time."

CHAPTER 31

THE trip home was slow, the pace set by the walking wounded among them. Gabrielle spent long hours wedged into a cart with Derkh or another of the grievously injured men and more time in the evenings working with the other bonemenders. By nightfall she was stiff and weary, more than ready for sleep.

Still, she found time to walk with Tristan and give him a full account of Jerome's death. This time she was able to tell it with more sorrow than shame, and Tristan's heartfelt reaction comforted her as much as Haloan's wise words.

"He wasn't alone, then. Thank the gods," said Tristan. His voice roughened with emotion. "All this time I imagined the two of you, each dying alone and uncared for on that bloody field. It filled me with horror." He stopped walking and turned her by the shoulders toward him, his blue eyes serious for once. "You shouldn't have gone back, Gabrielle. It could have been the death of you. But thank you. Thank you for staying with him and easing his passage."

They walked on awhile in silence, until Tristan began humming in time to their steps. Gabrielle recognized the tune as one they had sung at FirstHarvest. "That seems a long time ago," she offered.

But Tristan didn't hear. He was lost in his thoughts, his eyes far away. A second later he said, "Sorry. Did you say something?"

"So long ago I've nearly forgotten," Gabrielle replied, amused. "Wandering the clouds, were you?"

Tristan was only a little sheepish. "I was thinking about Rosalie, if you must know. Maybe it's seeing you and Féolan together; it makes me wish I'd been more serious with her."

Gabrielle felt a pang of guilt. She had not told Tristan yet of her birth, and she hated to keep it from him. It was for Solange to hear it first, though. "How is it between you and Rosalie, anyway?"

"I wish I knew," Tristan replied glumly. "Her father whisked her back to Blanchette when we first started mustering—thought it would be safer. She could be married by now."

"Now that seems unlikely," Gabrielle chided. "For one thing, I shouldn't think there are too many marriageable men in Blanchette these days. Didn't they all come up with Dominic to defend Chênier?"

Tristan seemed cheered at the thought. He turned to Gabrielle with a wheedling grin. "You could put in a good word for me with her father. Tell him, you know, how responsible and serious I've become."

Gabrielle resisted the temptation to tease him. "I doubt you'll have any shortage of people to put in a good word for you, Tris," she said.

DERKH WAS SILENT AND GUARDED, perhaps with good reason. He got his share of dark looks from the soldiers who passed them by. It was one thing to give downtrodden Greffaire peasants free passage through the Basin lands, quite another to shelter the son of the invading commander. Tristan made a point of walking by Derkh's cart, and the men of his unit followed his lead. In this way the boy's presence gained grudging acceptance.

Féolan, however, was constrained in the young man's company, and he knew very well why. Col's death lay between them, a malevolent unseen presence. He said nothing until Derkh regained some strength. Then one evening when the others were hunkered around a fire, he asked him for a private audience. The road skirted the river here, and it was but a short walk to a sloping granite bank. Here Féolan pulled out his sword, laid it at the astonished boy's feet and knelt before him.

"Féolan. What is this?" Derkh's voice was unsteady, for he recognized the action.

"I owe you the blood-price, Derkh." Féolan had learned the term in *Gref Oris*, and though the concept was savage, he could think of no other atonement that would satisfy a *Gref Orisé* citizen. "It was I who killed your father. I fought him fairly, face to face. Still, I am sorry for the grief I have caused thee."

He looked up at Derkh in utter seriousness. "If you wish to kill me, I will not resist." It was a deadly gamble, but Féolan believed he had read the boy's character aright. He waited.

For one moment, Derkh was a breath away from snatching up the sword. Justice, his mind clamored. You shall have justice.

But it wasn't justice, was it? Rather it had been justice for Féolan to kill an invader. He thought of Gabrielle, who had healed him not for fear of her life but out of simple compassion when it would have been "justice" to let him die.

With a shaky hand, Derkh picked up the sword and passed it back to Féolan. "Take it," he said thickly. "It is my father who was the cause of..." He gestured back up the road. "It shames me to have been his son."

"Nay, Derkh," said Féolan softly. Here, he thought with a twist of pity, was another painful burden, one no boy should have to carry. "Hear what I say now," he said, switching to *Gref Orisé* speech and laying a hand on Derkh's shoulder. Derkh would not meet his eyes but did not shrug him away. "Your father's actions, I doubt not, were true to his beliefs. From what I saw of your land, there is no great leeway given in the matter of beliefs. But Col was a courageous and loyal warrior, and he followed his duty as he saw it. You may disagree with his actions. But you need never be shamed at your parentage."

He never quite remembered how it happened that Derkh was pressed against him, crying in great gasping sobs that wrenched his thin shoulders. It didn't matter. Féolan held him until he was done, and thus was their friendship sealed.

BETWEEN FÉOLAN AND GABRIELLE too, a strange tension hung. It began imperceptibly, but seemed to Gabrielle in the latter part of the journey to grow with every step they took toward Chênier. The delight they found in each other's presence became muted, their silences awkward where once they had been full of ease. Their conversation was careful, not quite so freely spoken from the heart.

Her own uncertainty for the future was the cause. As she neared her home, it loomed over her, pulling her in too many directions. She did not know how to speak of it to Féolan, and it made her withdrawn and oversensitive.

They were about a day and a half from Chênier when Féolan raised the matter directly. They were having a rare meal alone. Tristan was eating with the men of his unit. Derkh, who walked or rode Arda for short distances now, still tired quickly and was dozing in the shade. Féolan returned from the cook tent with a distinctly unappetizing menu—cold stew from the night before and a round of stale flat bread. Looking at the congealed gray broth in her bowl, Gabrielle wrinkled her nose. "Nasty."

"Enough to turn one altogether against Human cookery," Féolan agreed.

Gabrielle flared, the humor lost on her. "This sludge is not 'cookery,' and you know it. There's nothing wrong with the food I was raised on!" She dug her spoon into the ugly-looking stew, raised it to her lips—and could not make herself eat it. What was wrong with her, snapping at an innocent jest? She set the bowl beside her on the ground and took a deep, deliberate breath before meeting Féolan's eyes. In them she read concern, not offense, and that unsettled her further, ready as she was to be angry.

"I'm sorry, Féolan," she said. "That was uncalled for." She didn't feel better, though. She felt "all in a turmoil"—her mother's expression.

There was a careful pause as they both searched for the words to put things right again.

"Is it well with thee, Gabrielle?" asked Féolan, lapsing into the more formal speech that came naturally to him at serious moments. "You seem … "

"I know I haven't had much time for you," she cut in. "But I have to put the patients first." She had declined to resume leadership of the bonemenders, content to leave it with Manon, who had done an admirable job in her absence. But she had still taken on full duties.

"I know you do," he said quietly. "A calling is not a thing that can be set aside on a whim. And I was not about to complain about the lack of your company, well though I would love more of it."

"I would too," confessed Gabrielle. She felt calmer, her defensiveness falling away. They had had so little chance to be alone together.

"I was going to say, you seem worried. Though I'm not sure that is quite the right word. Is it near the mark?"

It was. Suddenly the bottled-up words came out in a rush. "So much in my life has changed, Féolan, with no chance to understand it. I have not even properly mourned my father yet. And what will come after? I try to imagine what our life will be, and I cannot see it. Am I to leave Gabrielle behind and become Twylar? My family is still my family, no matter my birth. And my work ... It's not conceit, I don't think, to say that these people—my people—need me in a way the Elves do not. When I made my vows, it was them I promised to serve ... "

She paused, searching for her next words. "Your home is so beautiful and its people also. There could be happiness for me there, I think. But Féolan, am I to turn my back completely on Verdeau?"

She had not glanced at him once while speaking, determined to say it all, whatever his reaction. Now she was surprised to see him looking so unperturbed. He laughed out loud at her obvious relief.

The horns sounded, and they were on the road again before Féolan spoke.

"Perhaps you'll want to live in Chênier still, or spend half of each year there," he mused. "Many Elves divide their time between two settlements where they have close ties. My own parents have been several years now in Moonwash settlement, visiting my mother's people.

"Or maybe," he smiled, "the role of First Ambassador will be a real position now, and we will travel the roads of the Basin together, you mending the sick while I conduct terribly important talks with terribly important people."

Gabrielle thought of Féolan's parents, away "visiting" for years rather than weeks, and understanding blossomed within her.

"We have time, Gabrielle," Féolan said, reaching out to fold her hand in his. "Time to experiment and see what feels right. Time to find a life that welcomes us. You don't have to hurry your path."

They did have time, more time than Gabrielle had ever imagined. The road ahead was long, but for now she need only see as far as the next destination. And that was easy.   .

She was going home.

photo credit: Wayne Eardley

Holly Bennett is the Editor-in-Chief of Special Editions at *Today's Parent* magazine where she has worked for seventeen years. Her best qualification for writing *The Bonemender* is all the fantasy that she has read aloud to her children. (*The Lord of the Rings* three different times!) She read pages from her manuscript aloud to her youngest son at bedtime. "Aaron was my first editor," she says. "He said to me one night, 'You know, Mom, you use the phrase "smiled grimly" an awful lot.' And he was right; I had!" Holly lives with her family in Peterborough, Ontario.